DRAG THE DARKNESS DOWN

a novel by

MATT BAKER

NO RECORD PRESS
BERKELEY, CA | ITHACA, NY
WWW.NO-RECORD.COM

Design and layout by No Record Press
ISBN-13 978-0-9789808-9-4
ISBN-10 0-9789808-9-1

Matt Baker was born in Indiana and raised in Kansas. He attended the University of Arkansas and the Players Workshop of the Second City. He won the Fastest Typist Award in the eighth grade. His work has not been translated into any languages. He lives in Little Rock.

Angela Marklew once flipped her car ten times and used to test explosives for the Canadian government. Bored of blowing things up, Angela has commenced a massive photographic study of forgotten areas in the American Southwest. Risking violent encounters in Nevada, dehydration in New Mexico, even becoming the lone victim in a near fatal car accident, she seeks to capture scenes of emptiness and decay from the extreme marginalia of reality to tell an incomplete narrative that leaves as much hidden as shown. She can commonly be found scaling broken ladders, jumping fences and wading in swamps in search of the next broken tractor or abandoned prison. Angela's work has been exhibited in Ottawa, Eastern Québec, Louisville, San Diego and Los Angeles. Her portfolio can be viewed at http://www.fstopinertia.com and she can be contacted at angela@fstopinertia.com.

No Record Press publishes literary fiction. Visit us online at www.no-record.com.

There is no Frothmouth, Arkansas. There is a Little Rock, a Fayetteville, a Kansas City, and a Memphis but I've altered the details to suit my purposes.

This book wouldn't exist without the support from family and friends: Mom, Dad, Karleen, Jennifer, Sinclair, Ali, Courtney, Wil, Skip, and Miles.

For my family

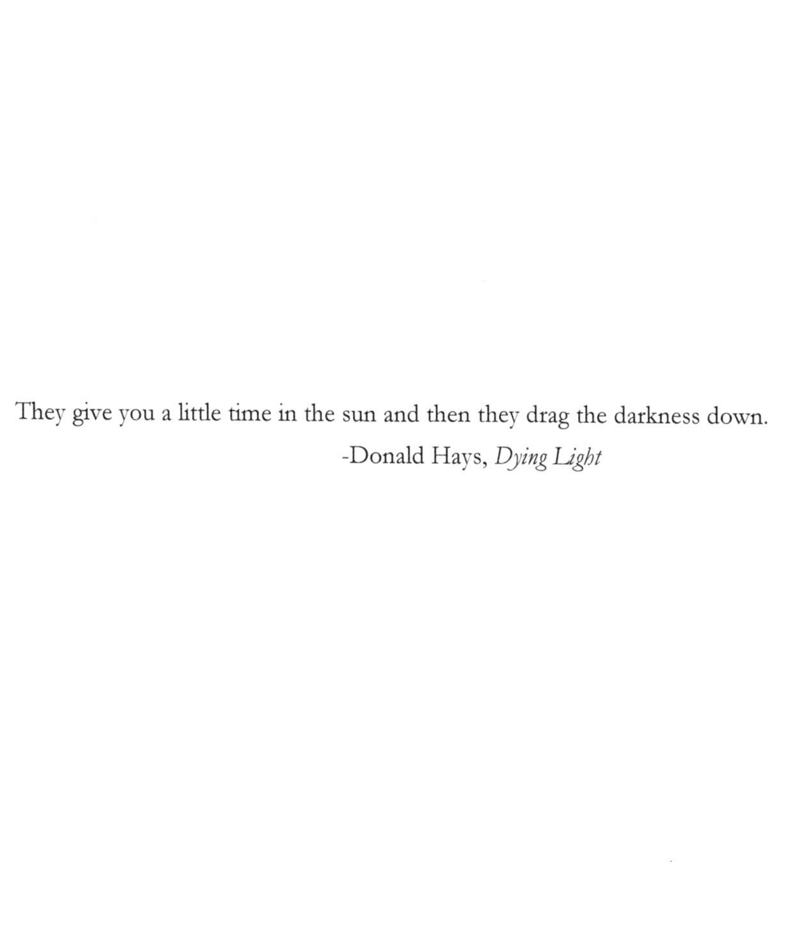

They give you a little time in the sun and then they drag the darkness down.

-Donald Hays, *Dying Light*

ONE

Chapter One

MY NAME'S ODOM SHILOH. My sister's name is Bridget although we call her Birdshit. That's what we've called her for thirty-six years. When she was a baby, learning to talk, she could never quite get her name out of her mouth the way it was intended. "Birrgdshit," is what it sounded like she was saying, so we started calling her Birdshit. Even schoolteachers and neighbors got in on it, somewhere along the way failing to realize that the tail end of her name was, in fact, a less than desirable word to spout in public. It's all right though. We're small town folks in an even smaller town and we do things our way, always have, and probably always will.

So my sister ran off, out of Frothmouth, with a black boy from around here. She ran away with him to north Louisiana, we think. Thirty-six years old and not married ever a once, not even any kids to boot; she falls for this eighteen year-old boy who tied for second in the state in total high school rushing yards last season. Every coach that's ever seen him run agrees: that boy's sure got a future in front of him. But he's on probation for fraudulently registering his car; he couldn't go away to any of the big football schools to play ball. So theoretically he was supposed to stick around Franks County for a year, pumping through flat rubber tires while his probation officer watches, whistle between teeth, at the end of the course. But then this boy, he glances to one side, spies Birdshit alone in the grandstand. He stops jumping through them bureaucratic hoops, skips town instead. And now the two of them are in Louisiana. At least we think they're in Louisiana. But I don't know any more than that right now.

I got me a buddy, Blakey Flake, who is from Louisiana, the center part; he knows everything from Alexandria on up to the Arkansas border; knows the roads, and all the creatures that live there. We're going to go find Birdshit and put her back in her cage, you could say. Back to Momma's house where she's been living her entire life, minus that five week stint when she tried living on her own. That stint didn't work out too well. But that stint's a story I don't need to get into right now.

We get to driving. Blakey Flake does all of it. He flew up to Little Rock earlier today at my request. I picked him up in my Honda Accord of the year 1997; he told me to scoot it over and let him drive. I asked him to be careful. I'm sentimental about the '97 Honda: four doors, four cylinders, green. It's got the usual dings and a deep dent over the left rear wheel where a bicyclist ran into me in downtown Memphis.

Actually, the reason I'm a little touchy with the '97 is that it's technically a crime scene. It's a small matter, I hope. That bicyclist was hurt pretty bad, that's what the papers and television are saying. He's a professional cyclist from France. His name is Pierre Duponte. He's in the hospital with several broken bones in both legs, a shattered shoulder, a sprained wrist. They are awaiting the results from further tests to see if he suffered brain damage. His safety helmet split in half when his head hit the ground. They said he was traveling at top speed when the impact happened. I didn't even realize it was an organized race that I was driving through. I figured it was your typical Saturday morning cycling club full of scrawny, bald, suburban white guys. But their bikes were something else, I couldn't take my eyes off of them. They looked like heavyweight champions: strong, agile, awesome. I got so engrossed in watching how they were able to move so swiftly that I soon found myself aware of nothing else. I felt it first, the noise came second—I'd hit something.

In retrospect it's unclear who was technically at fault. I didn't stick around to find out though. I darted down several side streets, hopped on I-40 and sailed across the Mississippi River back to Arkansas as fast as I could. I knew Pierre was hurt but I was scared. I don't need the police putting the light on me in those little rooms. I don't want them prodding me about the past, the family, or the woods.

I admit. I've been out of sorts lately. I've been having these fits where I zone out and lose track of things happening around me. On three different occasions I've awoken from some kind of semi-conscious state to find myself driving with no destination or ability to recall what led to my road trip. One time I got as far as

Arkadelphia before I snapped out of it, idling outside a gas station, listening to two Spanish girls gossip about their boyfriends. It wouldn't be too hard to end up in Memphis. It's only an hour and ten minutes away.

In fact, this going to get my sister is probably a wholesome distraction for now. It doesn't feel half bad to get away from Frothmouth. I was never one for taking vacations. After all, you always got to go home. You wonder what sense there is in deluding yourself for a few days or a week when home is always back there, waiting, and ready to crash down on you. No point in getting away unless you're going away for good.

I can't get away. Frothmouth, my house, step-son, soon-to-be ex-wife, Momma, my Birdshit, that's what I got. Even if I could gather up all the strength I've ever been capable of that still wouldn't be enough for me to just get up and walk away for good. The most mysterious forces aren't way out there, millions of miles away, invisible and star destroying. No cosmic eagle wings beating the vacuum at the core of the universe, scattering moon-sized asteroids like cigarette ash out the window of time. That's maybe how Birdshit would describe it in one of her poems. I think what it means is that the most powerful forces in the universe are those closest and most familiar.

If you can find Little Rock, Arkansas on a map you're pretty close to where our town is. Go east on I-40 to where the hills turn into flatlands and that's where we are, all 327 of us. It was 328 last month but old man Mr. Cohen finally died of a heart attack, after surviving the first five. He'd lived by himself and no one ever remembered him as a young man. In fact, it got people to scratching their heads sometimes wondering how old he really was; no one could remember him as anything other than bald, shriveled and permanently bent forward.

Frothmouth's like most small towns, I guess. There's Garner's Gas & Snack where most of the town's gossiping and social gathering takes place. Old man Mr. Garner still runs it by himself with only the occasional help from his drunken son, David. It's where I go every morning to buy a newspaper. Sure, it's got some other buildings I'm happy to stay away from: the dive bar, the police station. The dirt roads tangled up in the woods like hair. Those I do drive a lot.

Birdshit and I've lived here all our lives. We grew up in a green house surrounded by the woods that thrive in the northwest corner of the county, woods that absorbed all of our secrets. There's a beautiful little pond buried back there. Not many people know about it. It's hard to find. I like sitting down on the bank and watching that water breathe in and out, center to shore, very slowly, like it always has. Before any of us were here and long after we're gone them woods will remain. Everything they've witnessed, carved into its natural history. The I-love-you's and old treehouse ladders leading to nowhere. All my life the silhouette and the glare and watchful eye of them knotholes has followed me. The tree-branches draped over you, gripping the ground with shadows. Every morning it's a reminder of something. Something I spent my twenties thinking about and my thirties trying to forget.

Now before I go any further and before we even cross over into Louisiana, I got to tell you the truth of the matter is I ain't going after my sister because she's with a black boy. No, sir, that don't make a lick of difference to me or anyone else in our town. It's too bad people naturally accuse. It's the ones who accuse who still imagine black men dangling up in the trees.

In fact, Frothmouth is the only town in Franks County that has a black executive branch. Mayor Ferguson has been our leader for twelve years now. He's local, born and raised in Frothmouth, graduated from Philander-Smith over in Little Rock. He went to law school somewhere up in Ohio. He's the most educationally decorated person in Frothmouth. He talks about logical fallacies and poetic leaps of faith. Every Sunday night he cooks up a huge soul food dinner and everyone in town is invited. Most folks try to swing by and get themselves a plate; by the time the night is through it's not unusual for two hundred people to have made their way through the serving line.

Down this way the blacks used to have this saying. And for the life of me I can't remember it exactly but it goes something like this: The Southern white man will let you live close but won't let you live high. The Northern white man will let you live high but he won't let you live close. Now that's about a wash if I ever heard one.

Through the years we've managed to expel most of them violent combative racist types up north where they belong, to live their segregated lives amidst talk of peaceful reconciliation and Christian harmony. Hell, they're nothing but a bunch of R.O.T.C dropouts wearing camo and sitting high up in leafless trees in the middle of January, freezing to death with a crossbow laid across a branch talking about state rights, gun laws, immigration and patriotism. Down here, we just find it hysterical to watch on the TV. It's better than "COPS." Okay, once in a while we hang our dirty laundry out for some media airtime: let a few white-robed hooligans swagger out of the forests, lugging their burning crosses behind them like the ghosts of suicide bombers. They stand out in pharmacy parking lots with a megaphone and scream about brimstone. These were the guys at the back of the high school table blighted with acne scars and banished from the greener side of the bell curve, and their actions are like so many compressed "fuck you's" uncorked and sprayed by the Northern underclass across the iron guts of its subway stations.

No, we have much more important reasons for our urgent need to return Birdshit quietly and safely home. It's long, complicated, sad. But I don't need to go into that right now. I'd rather find her first, and explain later.

We get to putting some miles on the '97 when Blakey finally takes a cigarette out of his mouth long enough to try and make conversation. Blakey Flake is missing a few teeth from the cigarettes, a pinky finger from his oil rig days, and plenty of hair that he hasn't seen since the early morning of his twenties. He looks normal enough without it though. I'm just glad he doesn't comb over the hair on the side of his bald scalp into a fancy bow. Sometimes I fool myself into thinking I'm still young enough to change the course of my life. Blakey's forty eight years old, nine years older than I am. He's not fooling anybody.

"You know where you going, Blakey?"

"Oh yeah, got me a little eagle eye who tells me that sister of yours is in Bonita."

"That in Louisiana?"

"About five jumps from the border."

Blakey Flake's got him a whole gathering of eagle eyes, as he calls them. His eyes call him the Bald Eagle, and they're not joking. He's a State of Louisiana certified and licensed private investigator. A fifth career, he calls it, his final stop on the employment merry-go-round. Prior careers saw him working on oil rigs, teaching community college art appreciation classes, delivering transplant organs and stealing cars. You're probably wondering how the State of Louisiana gave him a P.I. license if he used to steal cars. And you're probably thinking he never got caught. But he did get caught, big time; got caught in Shreveport trying to outrun two of those sleek Camaro highway patrol cars. He couldn't get the Dodge Colt he'd stolen out of second gear, the clutch was stuck and the engine overheated. Finally it blew up and threw Blakey out of the car into a ditch. They took him to county jail and fitted him into what they thought would be a permanent orange jumpsuit and cheap rubber flip-flops. At his trial, which he demanded—opting out of a plea deal which would have sent him to prison for three years—he represented himself. He wrote his responses in prison pencil and swapped cigarettes for stamps. At trial he put on a show. He'd cite rules that hadn't been on the books since Napoleon was busy scribbling the code; on the stand he pleaded the fifth to every single question; he cross-examined witnesses with questions like, "Suppose you bought a baby parrot and taught it to swear. When it starts swearing of its own volition, is it taking the Lord's name in vain, or are you?" During closing arguments he stood up and told the jury, "I have two graduate degrees from Tulane," (he only had one) "and graduated tri-cumma lauda-dauda from Louisiana State University." (missed the grade cutoff) "Go Tigers." (never been to an NCAA game in his life). "I taught Survey of Art in the Western World at Middle Louisiana Community College;" (this was true) "I'm not a career criminal. I confess, I tried it out. I failed. I'm done. You see the thing about me that is different is that I have options. Your average criminal kind don't have college degrees. He's stuck in a life of crime. Where's he gonna go? Go get him a real job, hell no, he ain't. But, I am. I got me a fancy resume printed up, suits, ties and recommendation letters and a reference sheet a mile long, which includes congressmen, senators, business owners, you name it, even the offensive coordinator of the L.S.U. Tigers. You see, I'm going places. Don't let this little setback get in the way of my bright future."

Earlier in the proceedings, the prosecution had brought in an art expert from a rival institution who questioned his credentials. But it did little to dampen Blakey's momentum. He knew that first impressions were priceless, but last impressions were the ones worth money. So for his finale he held a copy of a Seurat painting, the one with the people picnicking and sitting in the grass. "Lookey here," he said. "See this? It's a pretty painting, ain't it? Look closer." Then he took deliberate, painfully slow steps closer to the jury. "Looking different, huh?" He invited the jurors to look even closer until he had the painting right up against their noses. "See, this here's called pointillism. Its perspective changes, right? From back, it looks one way. From up close, it looks different.

"You see, I'm just asking you to look closely and pay attention to the dots. Not the bigger picture. The bigger picture, this case, is messy and ridiculous. Right? You follow? Good. Now, if you just take the time to look closer, you'll see that I'm not guilty. And don't forget, most importantly, and I cannot stress this enough. Jesus, our savior, is in the details, right? And I quote from that good, good book: "If thou hath sins commit, then our Lord savior Jesus acquits."

The prosecution started saying something to the judge, but the jury, who most certainly held the highly popular idea that non-believers are forever guilty as believers are divinely forgiven, were already nodding in a near-choreographed manner, murmuring, "Amen."

Acquitted.

As a P.I., Blakey's forte is monitoring unfaithful husbands. His business card plainly states that his expertise lies in "Intimate Resolution." He makes a solid income for himself, following around jolly-dicked husbands. Blakey takes videos, snapshots and uses sound recording devices to collect evidence. He even employs beautiful Kappas from Louisiana Tech in Ruston. They work on a contract basis; he reports them on his taxes. The thing about them young girls is not what you see or what you think you see, it's the way they smell. There's this sweet air that surrounds only them, that can lure a successful auto parts store owner with a rosy -cheeked wife and a gaggle of kids into a cheap hotel already garnished with cameras. But he isn't limited to this. He also, on occasion, helps the local police departments and various state investigative agencies in rounding up the state's no-goods, including a 78 year-old crystal meth kingpin, a cross-eyed granny rapist and a habitual drunk driver who has passed every field sobriety test administered but routinely blows a .38 B.A.L.

So here we are: me and the best P.I. in all of north-central Louisiana, who happens to be a very close personal friend of mine. He says this'll be wrapped in days, if not hours. I say this thing has only begun.

Chapter Two

AND WOULDN'T YOU KNOW IT but Blakey gets himself upside down on his directions, thinking Highway 133 is 52 or 165 or something like that and so instead of being in Bonita, we're in Bastrop. We get ourselves pulled over; Blakey executing a U-turn in front of a camped out state patrol car. Blakey rolls down the window, waits, lights a cigarette and waits some more. The highway patrolman stays in his cruiser for a solid three minutes.

"This car ain't stolen is it?" Blakey says.

"What do you think?"

Finally, the cop begins the walk from his car to ours. We both watch in the rearview. I put my hands in my lap and look at them.

"Howdy there, Bandit," the patrolman says.

"Yes, sir, howdy to yourself."

"No U-turns allowed back there."

"I know that now."

"You a fast learner, Bandit?"

"Yes, sir."

"Good, learn this: an illegal U-turn in the State of Louisiana costs one hundred and fifty dollars."

"If you say so," Blakey says.

"Not only do I say so, but I'll show you."

"Well, that's nice of you." Blakey says.

The patrolman walks back to his car.

"Where's he going?"

"Writing you up a ticket," I explain. I reach into my pants and pull out my wallet. "Where are we? What county?"

"I don't know," Blakey says. "Why?"

"Because..." I flip through the cards, the notes, everything in my wallet.

"What are you looking for?"

"I have it here somewhere."

"Have what, Odom?"

"There's got to be one. I know people. We know people, Blakey. But the cop can't know who I am. Understand?"

"Sure, whatever you say."

"I'm serious, Blakey. If he asks, I don't have any I.D. on me."

"Then how do you explain that?" He points at the mess in my lap.

"It's not anything, Blakey. You didn't even see it. You understand?" I drop the glove compartment open and cram my wallet and its contents into it.

The patrolman comes back to the car.

"I need your driver's license so I can write this up. That's a hell of a bump you have on your car. Is that from an accident?"

"No," I say, leaning over into the police officer's view, "it just happened."

"How did it just happen?"

Blakey looks at me like it's a good question. He doesn't know the truth. "I drove to Dallas to see Social Distortion in concert and when I came out when it was over, I realized someone had hit me."

Blakey hands him his driver's license and says, "You know, Jesus would have given me a warning,"

"I don't care if Jesus would have given you a handjob."

Blakey informs me that this is going under the miscellaneous expenses column in his invoice to me—services rendered in helping to find my sister. I've hired him on, remember. This is part helping out a friend, part making some money in the process. It seems Blakey is more motivated by the latter. It shows in that Bible

-talk. That trial was his finest moment. He was genuinely scared; cigarettes are expensive in jail. But somehow his penchant for atheism has become blatantly obvious in much the same way as it is for those show-off Christians who wear Jesus crosses between their breasts to advertise their affiliation. I've always found the worst Christians to be the very ones who wear those little crosses. Blakey's not much of a fan of the Christians. His motto, as he likes to remind me is: "Live it, quit talking about it." And he likes to point out that we can't live this so-called Christian life, so what we do instead is sit around and endlessly talk about it and pat each other on the back. Every year during Easter week he likes to drive around and find the folks taking turns dragging a cross around town in an alleged re-creation of Christ's miserable walk. He pulls up next to them and says, through a megaphone, "Why don't you take the wheels off that thing you asswipe."

The cop corrects our directions and we pull into Bonita, Louisiana and stop outside the Paved Street Café. It looks quiet enough; pretty much what you'd expect from a small town café. But Blakey tells me to stay in the Honda. He's got business to talk up. Some of his eagle eyes are meeting him here and he doesn't necessarily want me to lock my own eyes on them.

"They're undercover. I don't need you going and messing it all up," he says.

"I'm not going to mess anything up."

"These guys are on my taxes. My eyes and ears in the field."

"Your eagle eyes."

"That's right."

"But not your eagle ears?"

"Stop confusing the issue."

"I'm not confused yet."

"Listen. You don't understand. They've got code names. Eagle 1A, Eagle 2A. The numbers denote their identity and the letter corresponds with the operation. So for example, Eagle 1A today may be 1C tomorrow. See?" He shows me a spiral-bound memo pad. "It's all in there."

"I'm still not confused yet."

"Good. Stay that way. I'm going in. No watching where I go or nothing like that. These boys are waiting for me. I can see one of them right now, sitting in that window right there."

"Which one? With the red ball cap on?"

"Now, what did I tell you? You just forget what you'd seen. You hear me?"

"Erased."

Blakey gets out of the car. He lights a cigarette and stands for a moment surveying the scene. He seems to be waiting for something, like an actor offstage waiting for his cue. We're thirty yards from the Louisiana state highway we came in on and I don't see anything worth noticing, just us, the three trucks parked out front and this box-shaped building called the Paved Street Café. I shout from inside the car, "Blakey, get on in there."

"I'm going, I'm going," he says, throwing down his cigarette.

He's in the building for a total of eight minutes, according to the clock in my Honda. When he comes out, he shakes his head and lights another cigarette. After he lights it, he pulls it from his lips before inhaling and twirls it in between his fingers. I wave at him to hurry up and get in. He acknowledges me and holds a hand up to indicate he'll get in when he feels like it. The other guys remain inside the café. One of them peers out the window, watches me. Adjusts his red ball cap. When we make eye contact, he disappears. I mean, he ducks or steps out of the way, whatever it is private investigators do when they've been caught or someone is onto them. A few seconds later, I see the bill of his red cap emerge across the right corner of the window. I set my eyes on the window, waiting. Again, he sees me and disappears. This is getting old. Blakey flicks his cigarette into the darkness, gets in the car, finally, and brings with him the exhaust of a full flavor, bargain bin cigarette. At least name brand cigarettes smell good. I cover my mouth, cough, then realize I made myself cough for no reason.

"What's the word? You got my sister and her boyfriend tied up in there?"

"Afraid not."

"Well, what'd they say?"

"Said Birdshit and that black boy ain't here."

"Ain't here, where? Bonita?"

"Louisiana."

"They're not in Louisiana?"

"Nope."

"Then where are they?"

"Not far."

"Okay, then let's go."

"Actually Arkansas, just up the road."

"They're in Arkansas? Are you sure?"

"I have high confidence in my intelligence assessment."

"Your what? You just came out of a cheap eats shack in the middle of nowhere and you're talking about intelligence assessments? Where in Arkansas?"

"Little Rock."

"They're in Little Rock? The same Little Rock we just came from?"

"Yes, sir, I'd imagine it's the same one."

"So we have to drive back up there."

"I'd reckon if you want to find your sister and that black boy she's with."

"How sure are you that hawk eye and eagle eye and falcon fang or whatever they're called know what they're talking about."

"One of my boys in there called your Momma—"

"Wait a minute." I turn so Blakey can see nothing but me. "No one calls my Momma."

"Well, someone did."

"You listen to me good. I'm not gonna say it again. No one calls my Momma."

Blakey waits for me to settle. A long-haired man wearing a cook's apron drags a green trash can across the parking lot to a trash disposal bin. After a deep breath, I let go of it. "Okay. So go on. What happened?"

"Anyhow, they got your sister's cell phone number from your Momma, called it, play-acted to be someone else and got your sister to tell him she's staying with friends in Little Rock."

"Well if that ain't a burnt bite, I don't know what is. This isn't something you could have done yourself? Isn't there a standard checklist you do before you launch a full scale investigation, such as call phone numbers, check addresses, very basic stuff? We drove three hours to find out that my sister is three hours back the other way, the way we came from?"

"Pretty much."

"Pretty much. What an unbelievable answer coming from a professional like you. And I'm paying you for this?"

"We're friends too."

"Well how about doing this as a favor."

"I can't pay bills with favors or eat favors."

"Blakey, get out of the driver's seat. I'm driving us back to Little Rock before you get us another ticket or make another wrong turn or follow a bad tip and steer us off towards Tennessee."

Blakey lights a cigarette. I tell him to put it out, no more smoking in my car. He tosses it. I seat belt myself into the driver's side. Blakey doesn't buckle up. I pull the car up to the window of the Paved Street Café, wait a minute until the red ball cap wearing prick shows his face again. When he does, before he can jerk away, I hold up a big, fat middle finger.

Chapter Three

THE DRIVE UP TO Little Rock is quiet. I know Blakey is itching to ask me about my wife, Bree. He's heard the rumor that she's leaving me. He let it slip on the phone before he flew up here. I ignored it then, and he's left it alone ever since.

"So what's that ol' boy of yours Spark Plug up to?"

"You mean, Sparkman?"

"Yeah, whatever you call him. I haven't seen him in awhile."

"I don't think you've ever seen him."

"Y'all schooling him at home?"

"I think so. Sometimes."

"That's kind of the thing nowadays, right?"

"Homeschooling? It might be. Most kids I hear that are homeschooled come out pretty bright and really know their stuff. I don't know though Bree just likes it better this way."

"How come?"

"She thinks public schools are crap."

"They are where y'all live."

"I don't buy it. I think public schools are fine. I should know. I'm the Assistant to the Assistant Football Coach here."

"What's he look like? Wait, don't tell me. He looks like his mother, don't he?"

"Maybe a little."

"He looks like Bree, don't he? Just like her, like a little piece fell off her and grew into him."

"Well, Blakey, that's kinda how it works. A little branch so small you have to use a microscope, broke off inside of her and grew into a little human being."

"Yeah, I know that. I've got two graduate degrees…"

"…One."

"Whatever. Bree must be proud."

"I have no idea."

We stop and get gas and two times I pull over to the side of the road so that Blakey can smoke a quick cigarette. I was firm in not allowing him to smoke in my car. He whined that I had let him when he was driving us down to Louisiana. I told him that was when I had faith in him. That faith has been tested and while I consider allowing my faith a re-birth, I'm putting strict rules on the date of incarnation.

"I'm your friend, that's faith enough isn't it?"

"Blakey, anyone can screw up something as phony as faith. I'm taking off work, using vacation time to do this. I don't have days to waste following bad leads."

"Relax, buddy. And let's be perfectly clear. You don't even need to work. You could quit today and it wouldn't make any difference. You're a Shiloh. Froth-mouth High School isn't going to miss its Assistant to the Assistant Football Coach and second period study hall monitor if you never show up again. And we'll find her. I know it's important. Mistakes happen, that's the beauty of being human, you hear me? Just don't get all bent backwards. I tell you what, I won't charge you for today. Let's just keep all the bullshit to a minimum. Okay?" To further drive his point home, he pulls out his ledger and makes several large, sideways cutting, slash marks.

I keep driving. The state road winds through dark trees. The truth of the matter is that this world is fueled solely on bullshit. The sooner one realizes this fact the easier life will be. People look to the good in others and I know it's the bad that truly shapes this world around us. Those who choose not to accept this begin their lifelong dig, one granule at a time, into the elusive truth which hangs over all our heads like the sun. My daddy, a man I haven't seen or talked to in thirty years, knew too much and saw too much and that's why he disappeared.

"So no more about this," Blakey says.

His name is Sir Martin Shiloh and up until his departure in the year 1977 was the highest in command for the Shiloh family. I have no idea where the "Sir" is derived from but that doesn't matter. The point is, as he said, I've got it and once you've got it they can't take it away from you no matter who you are or what you did. The Shiloh family oversees a litany of business ventures and schemes, some legitimate, some not. The family fronts fraudulent non-profit foundations which have been able to acquire millions in grants and subsidies for phony projects. Many law enforcement agencies implicate my father as the founder of one of the foremost underground, anti-government, anti-democracy groups in America. The government—Red, White and Blue, Inc.—even tried hitching us to the Klan, but that allegation crashed and burned. No, the covert group to which Daddy belonged was an offshoot of the Shiloh family; something my granddaddy and uncles and no one else in the family for that matter were particularly fond of. I think they felt Daddy was going too far, spreading himself too thin maybe. But we all think that's why he's gone. The story goes that Red, White and Blue, Inc. fished him out of our hideaway farmhouse down in Lewisville. There's no telling where he is anymore. The year 1977 was a long time ago. I'd guess maybe he's still alive, but there's no telling what ol' R.W.B., Inc. can and will do. They could've shot him, sliced him up into a thousand pieces and fed him to the animals at the Little Rock Zoo or maybe the Omaha Zoo, which is supposed to be a nice one. Maybe they shipped him to a prison in Cuba. Maybe he escaped, and is smoking cigars with the communists.

Though I get to wondering whether he really is still alive. Especially when I'm driving by them woods, or sitting on Momma's back deck staring into them. I think I can see him sometimes and I wonder if he's been living out there all these years. Probably built himself a little mud and wood hut. Probably tamed himself a few wild dogs, trained them to go after wild boar; slits their throats after the dogs have them cornered somewhere. Probably hunts deer with an arrowhead he cut from rock, tied on the end of a long branch. He'd hide up in the trees, throw it through the neck of a naïve young buck.

"Besides," Blakey says, "It's the journey that counts."

Okay. There are a lot of pieces in between the beginning and ending of a story. Most people want to know the ending too fast. But I don't subscribe to the belief that the journey is the good part. Hell, the journey is usually long, slow and boring. I hear it picks up a little the older you get, around 50 or so, when you realize all those days and evenings spent in front of the television have yielded zero dreams accomplished. But until then it's sluggish. If you're lucky, and most of us aren't lucky, there are some real gems in there, along the way, on this journey you hear so much about, this journey of life. That's what they call it. That's what my father was after, the gemstones. And he found more high priced tidbits than he needed to know about; they just made him more curious and greedy, to keep on it, to keep finding and discovering the great truths about this world, the ones staring us in the face all along. So if you want to know the ending, this is it in many ways. He's gone and I haven't seen him since. Now it's over and Birdshit is gone. Did I not say the journey is boring and slow? Blakey and I haven't gone much further than the airport we started from. And that's where we are now, again, back in Little Rock, at Little Rock National Airport. We're sitting in the parking garage. It's quiet and safe. The hovering black helicopters can't see us here. You don't need a boarding pass to park. You don't even see anyone. A machine prints your ticket, and you give it back to the machine when you leave.

Blakey gets out of the car to smoke a cigarette. I'm tired already, watching Blakey stand there with his cigarette, smoking it proudly like its still the 1970s when smoking wasn't a crime. I know what he wants more than anything else in this world is for someone to care, though not necessarily about him.

I roll down the window. "Blakey, we need to come up with a plan."

"I'm thinking."

"You got an address for my sister?"

"You got a map of Little Rock?"

"No, but I know my way around a little."

"Know where 19th Street is?"

"Between 20th and 18th if I had to guess."

"That's where she is."

"19th Street? That's a great help. So we plan to hobble along 19th Street all day long hoping she pops out from behind a door and invites us inside for a cola and a peanut butter bar?"

"It's a start, ain't it?"

"Okay."

"They said 19th Street's close to downtown."

"Okay."

"That's all I know."

"How long have you been a P.I.?"

"Why?"

"Just wondering."

We make our way downtown. Blakey points out the Clinton Presidential Library and asks if we have time to take a quick tour. He says, "Clinton likes poetry just like your sister does. When he was in England as a Rhodes Scholar he walked around with a copy of William Blake's *Songs of Innocence and Experience* in his pocket."

"So does he have a title of nobility?"

"Well, he got a library built for himself. That's almost as good."

I tell him if we find Birdshit on 19th Street near downtown in the next thirty minutes then, yes, we can tour the Clinton Library, maybe buy some blueberries at the farmer's market, ride the yellow trolley over the Arkansas River and back again, whatever he wants.

"I'd like me a trolley ride," he says. "Been on the Memphis trolleys but not the Little Rock ones."

"Yeah," I say. "You seem like the trolley riding type."

From downtown we head south, crossing over the main east-west interstate that nicely divides the city into clear and understood halves: high crime and low crime. We make our way into the south portion of the city, roam through the Central High District, pass by the most famous high school in the country—Central High School—where them Federal troops had to show up with machine guns to get those black kids through the front doors. We find our way in the Quapaw District where most of the older homes in the city are situated, the stately and historic. If you remember that TV show, *Designing Women*, the opening shot is of a house down in here. The drivers are courteous and laid back. Turn signals are an option but it's no big deal. There's not enough traffic to really require that level of sophistication. When a light turns green, there seems to be a mandatory three-second pause before you're allowed to hit the gas.

I tell Blakey that we'll be coming up on 19th Street. He doesn't say anything so I glance over at him. He's looking out the window.

"What're you looking at?"

He's still staring.

"Blakey!"

I reach over and poke him with my finger and his head jerks up. "What?"

"Are you sleeping on the job, Blakey?"

"Nah, nah, just thinking."

"About?"

Several seconds pass and he turns to me. "About what?"

"You said you were thinking about something."

"I did?"

"You were sleeping you son of a bitch."

"Just dozed off, nothing special. Where are we?" He sits all the way up, reaches for his cigarettes and lighter, an innate instinct.

"We're on the moon, Blakey. We just drove by some historic footprints and a weathered flag still blowing away on a pole and I found myself a mess of golf balls. A shitload of them. I don't think them astronauts were doing anything up there, just playing damn golf the entire time. Set some records at the driving range, I believe."

We take a left at 19th Street and then a left on Spring Street, passing the governors mansion, his dwelling spread out to our right, surrounded by a fence.

"Well, well, governor lives like the captain of the ship in ol' Arkie."

"All governors live like this, Blakey."

"Except Reagan. He sold the Governor's Mansion, didn't he? Hell, why am I asking you? Anyhow, I'd say this has to be one of the top ships I've ever seen. Don't see no Birdshit yet, though."

"This almost seems pointless," I say. "It occurs to me that without any solid intelligence, we're doing nothing more than raking sand."

"Raking sand?"

"It's an old expression. My daddy used to say it."

"It must be pretty old because I've never heard it before. What's it mean?"

"An art history scholar, and you can't interpret a metaphor? You know, like repetitively doing something but not really getting anywhere."

"Is that right? Sounds kind of dumb to me. My own daddy used to say that he was born at night, but not last night. He also told me to never get involved with any woman whose name was Coco."

"That seems like strange advice. What was your mother's name?"

"Coco. Doesn't seem so strange anymore does it?"

"Your parents not get along?"

"Hell, they were barely together long enough to even make me. My birthday is in September, you see. Coco and my daddy met at a News Year's Eve party, got the motion going and that's how I came into existence. They married for the sake of my birth but within eighteen months they had split up. They shared custody."

"What was that like?" I ask.

"We don't have enough time to go into all of that. No sense in doing so either."

"So 19th Street is as much as you know? This is it."

I've completed a circle of sorts through the Quapaw District passing by where my sister used to rehearse with the Little Rock symphony. Since the symphony didn't have its own building they practiced in this historic house. It was built in the 1800s and has several tones of color on its exterior but in the back was a large room where most of the symphony members—minus percussion—could squeeze in and practice their songs. I dropped her off here many a time; I remembered that music, fast and loud and imposingly organized, coming from inside as I drove away. I stop in front of it and tell Blakey about the significance of the house. He says, "Yeah? I think I knew that." I wait to see if he says anything else. But he doesn't.

I pull away and stop at the intersection of 17th and Broadway. "I'd say we're in the neighborhood if everything you're saying is true. We can follow 19th going west, but going that way puts us further and further from downtown."

"Maybe we ought to park and walk around, ask questions, go door to door. Just like selling girl scout cookies or collecting donations for the S.P.C.A. Pull in here," he points. "I need to get me a drink and some more cigarettes."

The convenience store is busy. I park on the side, pulling up next to a gangsta-decorated Cadillac. The kid sitting behind the wheel can't be fifteen. His hat is worn crooked in the new crooked style, a miniature cigar fuming from his lips. I nod at him. He looks right through me like I never existed.

Blakey gets out first and I follow him inside. There's a line five or six deep.

He holds out a hand, "You got a picture of her?"

"My sister?"

"Yeah, who else?"

"No. I don't think so. Should I've brought one?"

"Wouldn't have hurt."

"Then why didn't you mention it before?"

"I just now thought of it."

The interior of the store is cold, bright and spotless. My eyes become starry and out of focus trying to decipher the enormous brand choice I have for sodas. Everywhere you go these are the same refrigeration units powered from the same energy plant which the same types of people will sell you. I find an orange colored can and hope the stuff inside tastes orange and get in line. There's a small deli counter in here, several racks full of clothes. Running down the middle of the store is a big table with foot-high sides packed full with 24-ounce cans of beer, all brands, peering out through the ice. Blakey grabs one and pops it open right there, takes a drink and gets in line in front of me. He turns around, smiles, drinks again. We move forward. The Arab guy behind the counter is saying, "…My friend, my friend, my friend, I understand but it is not the way you see it. Those lighters are eighty-nine cents, the small ones. The one you have, my friend, is a large one. You see? It is one dollar and nineteen."

"They haggling over the price of a Bic up there?" Blakey says.

The guy shakes his head, "Nah, nah, that ain't right." His dreadlocks sway like windchimes for the deaf, striking each other silently, as he continues shaking his head, walking out, disgusted and lighter-less.

Blakey gets up there sipping his beer. The Arab guy says, "You drink already," and smiles.

Blakey says, "When you get the thirst you gotta squelch it."

He says back, "When I get the thirst I drink Sierra Mist."

"Yeah, well, you wish you could drink this." Blakey lifts up the can, shows the label, then drinks it. "But you don't because they start taking away your virgins in your alleged afterlife for every swallow of booze."

"No, that is not correct. Alcohol will ravage our bodies and minds. That is why."

"Yeah, okay and give me a pack of the cheapest smokes you sell."

The Arab clerk sets a pack of smokes on the counter. It says "cigarettes" on it; nothing more.

"Not that cheap," Blakey says. "Y'all carry Nuggets here?"

"Yes," he nods. "A Nugget for you." He places the package on the counter.

"I say this is about the only place I ever been where I can buy a tall can of beer, a pack of smokes, a sandwich, a pair of expensive jeans and tennis shoes all in one stop."

"Yes, my friend, we offer a lot to buy."

"I tell you what I do admire is you Iraqis and your Islamic art. The Abbasid dynasty was a great period for y'all. Pottery, ceramics, metalwork. Very beautiful."

The clerk smiles. "I am not Iraqi. I am…"

"Y'all were like the Muslim Rome about a thousand years ago. Baghdad was a very hip place. Nowadays, shit, I don't know."

The clerk just smiles and holds out his hand, awaiting payment.

Blakey pays. Then I pay for my soda. We leave. The clerk bids us a good day.

We get in my car and I look down and notice for the first time how short Blakey's slacks are. Sitting in my car, his knees fully bent, the bottoms of his pants barely cover the top of his cowboy boots. If they were any shorter, I'd be seeing Blakey's white legs. These boots he has had as long as I've known him. "These here are my working boots," he says, after noticing my stare.

"I thought they looked familiar, that's why I was looking them over."

"Dandy style, ain't it?"

"Dandy style is what you are all about, sir."

"Damn, right, that and a hot, bent over and buttered piece."

"That too."

I think I would be a small time jerk if I said that in a world of quick assessments and generalizations, Blakey Flake would be a spitting image of the truck driver character in the Smokey and the Bandit movies. The character's name slips my mind, both real and fictitious. I believe he was a real life singer of some notoriety when I was a youngster. But he stands that height, with the same skeletal build and hard muscle wrapped around his limbs, in strings that give off a weathered and aged look—like his skin had been soaked overnight and dried in the hot sun. And the cigarettes have ruined his face. He smokes so much that I think he goes into withdrawals the moment he flicks an extinguished butt and starts to inhale normal air. Because that seems to be all it takes for him to light another one.

"You need to quit those, Blakey."

"Says who?" He inhales a slow drag, eyeing me.

"Says everybody. Where've you been for the last twenty years?"

"Been here, doing my thing, resolving intimate issues."

"Those things are going to kill you. You smoke what? Two, three packs a day?"

"Usually about three."

"Have you ever thought about quitting?"

"Sure, thought about it. Thought about screwing a blond-headed Finnish girl or a red-headed Irish girl with freckles sprinkled like cinnamon over her butt cheeks but I don't think that's going to happen."

"I bet if you tried to quit, you could. You could do anything you set your mind to."

"Is that some second period hall monitor wisdom?"

I pull into the pharmacy. I tell Blakey to sit still. I'll be back. He nods his head, rolls down the window and lights a cigarette. He hangs the cigarette out the window but the wind blows the line of smoke directly into my car. Blakey catches me watching and tries to fan it away like he gives a shit. I know he doesn't.

I walk straight up to the pharmacy counter. A middle-aged man of foreign distinction with a mostly bald head smiles carefully. My approach is quick, assertive, borderline hostile. I sense his guardedness. I smile and take my hands out of my pockets to reveal nothing that could be used in a robbery attempt. "Hello, may I help you?"

"Absolutely. I need patches, gum and pills."

"Excuse me?"

"You speak English?"

"Yes, I do. Very good English."

"Oh, okay, well, buddy of mine is trying to quit the cigarettes. I need the full treatment, anything that'll help."

"Well, sir, the nicotine gum and patches are over there in the glass case. I will have to unlock it for you once you find what you need. As for the pills, you will need a prescription."

"No kidding. Poor guy is breathing on one lung, with only thirty percent capacity at that and he needs to pay a doctor seventy-five bucks to write him a note that says he can buy a medicine that will drastically improve his health?"

"That is the way it works."

"Where've I been?"

"I do not know. Are you from around here?"

"About a score and fifteen miles, eastward. You know what a score is?"

"Is it like a point comparison, between two opposing teams?"

"Listen to you, talking big words on me. No, like four score and never mind. I think it's twenty but I'm not sure. I'm from Frothmouth. Heard of it?"

"Several times. On the ten o'clock news the weathercaster mentions a weather spotter there."

"That's right. That's Robert McCordery, our very own weather spotter. The guy is dumber than a roll of nickels but we don't bother telling him that, you know?"

"Why don't you look at the patches and gum in the glass case over there and I am sorry I can not help you with the pills." He turns around and arranges the prescription bags, all lined up in alphabetical order. The guy is so precise. For some reason I'm reminded about that ticket machine at the Little Rock airport.

"Your English is very good. I congratulate you. Where did you learn it?"

"Kuwait University."

"No kidding. They teach English in Kuwait?"

"Yes. Many people speak English in Kuwait."

"Really? Well, I may just have to go check it out then."

"Yes. It is a marvelous place to visit. We have desalination plants and resorts built into the ocean."

"Desalination?"

"Yes," the man says. "The barrel of oil, its dollar price rises to heaven in terms of your Cartesian graph. Because of this, we drink the ocean."

"I'm confused now."

"The world is very confusing. You must put your faith in God."

"I think we would pray to different Gods."

"God is everywhere, and always the same." He turns back around and crinkles the medicine bags.

I scratch my head, shake it and then scratch it again. "Seems like I remember these commercials all over the television talking about consulting your pharmacist for a sample."

He turns around. "No, you will need to go to a doctor to get a sample."

"That right?"

"Yes, that is right."

"You can give me a sample, can't you? I mean, what's the harm? What am I going to do, go sell quit-smoking pills on the black market? From the little I know about them, they make you a space cadet, your dick takes an hour to get hard and then shoots blanks at that. I can't imagine many folks desiring to overindulge with those kinds of effects."

"You are right about the side effects. And you seem as if you mean well."

"I do mean well. That's my life's intention, to mean well. I'm just trying to help out a friend. I'm being earnest and truthful."

"I understand now, I think. I do have several sample packages. They are not inventoried. They are the samples that we give to people who come in with a doctor's note for a sample."

He pulls open a drawer, grabs a folded-over cardboard box with pills in the see-thru pill casings. He tosses one at me. I catch it. "There you go, tell your friend to stop smoking on the second day. This sample will last only for two weeks. He should get started right away."

"Great. Now, how about them patches and gum."

I leave the pharmacy with a white paper bag full of smoking-cessation goodies. I get in the car and ask Blakey if he enjoyed his cigarette. "Cigarette? I've smoked two or three."

"Roll up your sleeve."

"What for? I ain't doing this."

"Just do it." I tear open the top of the box of patches. "Your sleeve isn't rolled up."

"I'm rolling, I'm rolling," Blakey says. I pull one of the patches out from its perforated home. It's wet and heavier than I expected. I slap it on Blakey's left triceps. He watches curiously and says it's cold.

"How do you feel?"

"Fine. Am I cured yet?"

"Not quite," I say, ripping open the nicotine gum box. I slice a hole through the plastic casing and pull out a piece in two parts and tell Blakey to chew on it.

"Abracadabra! You're cigarette-free, Blakey. Congratulations!"

"Don't I get some pills or something?"

"Not until you've eaten the most substantial meal of the day."

"I don't eat much."

"Well, we'll have you popping pills in no time. For now, though, let the patches and gum work their magic."

Chapter Four

BEFORE WE GO ANY FURTHER into nowhere, I have to get something to eat. I walk into Big Mouth Burgers and wait for someone to take my order. All the talk is in Spanish and for many seconds, maybe even a minute, it's like I'm not even there. They see me but that does not disturb their conversation. A pretty, dark-haired girl finally approaches. "Hola!" I say.

A few minutes later I come out of Big Mouth Burgers and the first thing I spy is Blakey smoking a cigarette. I run, at full speed, to the car, dropping my jumbo diet cola in the process. I slap the cigarette out of his hand; a shower of sparks and ash fall on his cowboy boots.

"No, no, no, Blakey. You can't smoke you dumb-dumb. That's why I got the patches and gum and the pills you take," I hold up a bag that contains his burger and onion rings, "after you eat this."

"Oh, I thought all of this was magic, like you said."

"It *is* magic, but you have to help it to work." I hand him his bag. "Here, eat. And smoke away, see if I care."

We sit in my car, windows rolled down, eating our lunch. A few homeless folks mill around the parking lot. They leave us alone. I give them the courtesy of a nod and this seems to be all it takes. Then from the entrance of Big Mouth Burger emerges a preacher-suited asshole. I had seen him at a booth, staring vaguely into space. Upon laying eyes on us he slowly approaches, waving a Bible over our car, looking upward, mumbling his words. Blakey and I exchange a look. "What the hell?" Blakey says, part of an onion ring falling on my seat, grease already burning into the leather.

"Can I help you?" I say, leaning a little out of my window.

"Blessing to you and your friend," he says, continuing with his act.

"Looks like you're blessing a Honda Accord of the year nineteen ninety seven if

I didn't know better."

"God blesses all, even Hondas, my friend."

"Right. Well, can you come back another time, like later, when we're not here to bless us?"

Up behind him comes a similarly dressed individual, although this one is half his age, maybe eighteen at most; polished skin, youthful looking to a fault. "What have you found here, Preacher Conway?"

"I've found me the Devil, I believe. The Devil's been here, I can feel it."

"I can feel it too, Father. This car is the Devil's handiwork. It was manufactured by the Japanese Buddhist engineers at Honda. Power windows and a faux-leather interior." I run my hands up and down, over the headrest. "Feel it, Father." I start laughing and Blakey points to his chest, indicating himself as the devil, an inside joke, an inside the car joke, but the all-knowing preacher has witnessed our carrying on. I can't take my eyes off him. Something about him holds my attention. Maybe it's the name: Preacher Conway. Seems like I remember his name mentioned in the same breath as Don Duggar, an old-time evangelical scam artist from the 1970s. I look at my hands, then put them in my pants, and start going through the cards in my wallet.

Conway walks over to the passenger side, face fixed in reprimand, bringing his Bible down from the holy heights, slapping it on Blakey's opened window as if an invisible, fly-sized demon had been rubbing its front legs together there.

"My son," he says, to Blakey.

"Son, hell no, bubba. I'm older than you by ten years at least."

"We're all children of God."

"If we're all children of God, then I'm the one that was born after God decided he'd had enough. The New Year's accident."

"Tell me, have you accepted our Lord Jesus Christ as your personal savior?"

"No, frankly I'm more a Spinoza kind of guy."

"Spinoza will not get you into heaven."

"You are surely right about that. But you know what, you can have it. You enjoy heaven all to yourself, don't worry about me."

"But don't you want eternal life?"

"Hell, no."

"But you have to want it."

"I don't want it."

"But, you have to. It's required. You're supposed to want to live forever. And then you have to beg forgiveness from Jesus Christ, and then he will grant it to you."

"Screw that. You can live forever, knock yourself out. I'll take sixty or so years and be happy with it, die tragically while storming into a motel room. The last thing I'll see is a naked young Louisiana Tech subcontractor straddling a bloated businessman. I'll tell him the jig is up and then I'll keel over. And I won't remember a damn thing."

"It's not that simple," Preacher Conway laughs, pleased with himself. "If you don't accept Jesus Christ, you go to hell after you die."

"Well, I'd imagine Spinoza is already there and waiting for me." Blakey takes a bigger bite of burger than he can manage, begins choking. A piece of meat falls out of his mouth. He picks up the piece and jams it back in. "I have some questions to ask him."

"Aren't you afraid of eternal damnation?"

"Nope." Blakey swallows, then pokes an onion ring past his lips, chewing on it slowly.

"Eternal torture and hell-fire. Doesn't that scare you at all?"

"Nope. I live in Louisiana. Not much scares me." Blakey continues to chew and examines an onion ring between his thumb and forefinger, the next one to be shoved into his mouth.

"There is no escaping hell. The Devil will have you for all of eternity."

"Okay."

The preacher fixes his eyes on me. "I see you've been watching me close young man, searching my words, searching for the Lord I suspect."

"That's not what I was looking for. Your work is finished here Father. I don't think the Holy Spirit has moved this man."

"And what about you, have you accepted Jesus Christ as your savior?"

"Oh, hell yeah!"

"Good for you."

"Thanks. Now, can you leave us alone, please?"

"Good day gentlemen," Preacher Conway says. "God is always watching, remember that."

"Okay," Blakey says, "you remember that too, next time you're alone with a little boy." Preacher Conway says something back, but I ignore him. Blakey is eating and not paying attention to anything but his onion rings.

Preacher Conway and his cohort stroll away from my vehicle. He raises his Bible again, high into the air, using it, it seems, as some sort of navigational device. He walks where the Bible takes him. He cuts through the parking lot and disappears between two abandoned, deteriorating buildings.

"I wish they would update these neighborhoods. These old buildings just crumbling away. It's too bad. Tax revenue."

"Tax revenue."

Blakey nods. Then says, "It's a sad world, ain't it?"

"How so?" I ball up my hamburger wrapper and toss it in the bag.

"People like that."

"Blakey, some people need that kind of stuff."

"Yeah," he says, folding up his wrapper. He finishes the last of his beer.

His cell phone rings.

I'm glad Blakey answers his phone because one of his eagle eyes was on the case. It turns out that Birdshit got suspicious after the anonymous call, so much so, she and her love-child bailed on Little Rock and headed north. This information came courtesy of one of Blakey's finest sets of eagle eyes, so he says. I asked where these fine field-op eyes were when we were driving around in circles and then why didn't *Blakey himself* make the phony phone call to Birdshit's cell phone to get her whereabouts, instead of some amateur. Blakey has nothing to say to me on those points except that he fully trusts his support network, both in the field and back at "headquarters." Although I have doubts whether or not an actual headquarters exists. If such a place does have existence then I can only imagine that it's in a crummy strip center, in a building that used to be a tanning salon back in the early 90s and still smells like oil, electricity and sweat. The card tables and folding chairs. The phone alone on the middle of a table. Some overweight woman with a beehive haircut and a box of Swiss cake rolls picking it up when it rings.

"Up north? Where to?" I say.

"En route to Fayetteville as we speak. Evidence is pointing to a friend of your sister's who is willing to put them up for a few days."

"What friend?"

"Margaret Kenzer?"

"Name doesn't ring a bell."

"You driving or you want me to drive?"

"I can drive to Fayetteville," I say. It occurs to me that my sister is actively on the run again. This is not the first time. She's spent her life running away, trying to escape. Before, it was intellectual. Now she's run off with one of the greatest Arkansas high school running backs in recent memory. With a boy who ran for over six hundred yards against Frothmouth High only last year. I can still see his metal cleats kicking up mounds of dirt, flashing in the sun. "My sister is on the run," I say.

"Yes, she is. She knows something."

"But how?"

"I don't know."

"Could've been your goofy eagle eye who got her on the phone earlier and led us here to Little Rock. He probably said something stupid."

"Doubt that. Your sister's a smart girl."

"No she ain't."

"You're smart, too, Odom. Hell, what's that language you speak?"

"I speak a little Spanish."

"See, that makes you smart. Your sister is a smart girl too. She plays classical piano, played with the Little Rock Symphony for a few years, right? She writes poetry. She's published a book."

"That doesn't make her smart, makes her talented. She's got impulse control problems. She's twenty seven thousand dollars in debt to the credit card companies. She's blind in one eye and hears a constant ringing noise in one ear. She drags her feet when she walks and chews with her mouth open. Her longest stint at a job was two months, as a bartender at Rodney Carson's place in Frothmouth. Remember how much of a disaster that was? Every boy that's ever liked her she ran away from."

"Yeah, but she's ambidextrous. She can write with her left and right hand at the same time. She can juggle. She can count backwards from one thousand in any increment you tell her to: by fives, sixes or seventeens. And not to mention she's pretty."

Indeed, she is the prettiest girl to ever have been born in Frothmouth. At one soul food dinner, Mayor Ferguson told her she had buttery brown hair like maple syrup, and eyes so radiant that men are left stupefied in their tracks after exchanging a single glance. He said her feminine curves are so finely tuned that only a German automotive engineer could have designed them; that her movements swell with so much sexual longing that men have been witnessed falling to the ground in agony. She nodded at him, too. In fact, for a while she considered calling a forthcoming book of poetry *Modern Day Medusa.* But I'm not sure what came of that notion. Momma tells her all the time that she's too pretty to be living with her. Thirty-six years old and getting older by the second. Momma reminds her that she's got no high school diploma, no education, no mental stability, just a few talents. None of which really mean much. "Time to cash in your pretty-card and get yourself a husband," Momma says, "'fore no man no longer wants your goods."

"I don't need a man," she always tells Momma. "At least not the kind of man you want me to get."

I tell Blakey we're going and navigate my Honda of the year 1997 northward towards Fayetteville. I set my cruise control at seventy five miles an hour and sit back and listen to Blakey smack his nicotine gum and watch him replace his nicotine patch out of the corner of my eye. When I ask him how he is feeling he says he doesn't know and that he isn't really feeling one way or another about anything. "Yeah," I say, "It sounds like you got so much nicotine onboard your little brain cells are dancing lullabies in their sleep."

"Yeah." Then after a minute of complete silence he says, "I been to Fayetteville once before. Long time ago, with my wife. We'd gone up there to hear a band play. I can't remember the name, some punk rock group she really liked. I was drunk though. I don't remember much. That was back when I used to drink a lot."

Blakey stares straight ahead.

"You still drink a lot, Blakey."

"Well, not as much as I used to. Back in the day I'd go buy two Budweisers—one for the store, one for the road. You don't see me drinking now do you?"

"Point taken."

"So anyhow, Fayetteville. Forget about how long it's been. Didn't you go to the U of A?"

"No. I went two semesters at Arkansas State in Jonesboro."

"You went two semesters and I got two degrees. Go figure. A Masters degree from Tulane," Blakey says, "the most educated P.I. in the history of private investigative services, I'd imagine. An M.A. in Art History with a double emphasis—Pre-Columbian and Postmodern Abstract."

"What is postmodern abstract?"

"Hell, if I know. That's why you get degrees in this stuff, because no one knows. It's a way to pretend you know. That's all we are Odom. Pretenders. Human beings are pretenders. We have not yet achieved our true essence, so we pretend."

I pass two trucks carrying chickens and another one hauling brand new German cars. The cars are stacked so carelessly I hold my breath until I'm sure one won't fall on us. I get the Honda up to ninety just so I can get around them. After I pass, I get back over in the right lane and let off the gas a bit.

"How's the family, Odom?"

Trying to get me to talk about Bree.

"I don't know."

"What do you mean?"

"The little shit's getting to the age that he's asking a lot of questions."

"We've all been there. It's a normal part of growing up. But it is a burden. I mean, when and how do you tell your kid what to say to people like that preacher Conway, who holds his Bible like a dowsing rod and his brimstone sermons like a death threat, offering gimmicky shortcuts, grandstanding about divisive belief systems that damn outsiders and offer guarantees only for those who belong. Well, anyone with a dozen or more synapses firing in their skull knows there are no shortcuts, life offers no easy paths, except for a very few of us. And it don't take long to look and realize you ain't one of them lucky ones. That's right, no guarantees in this life or any so-called afterlife. The best we can hope for is to maintain things the way they are for as long as we can. Stay out of harm's way as far as we're able. Repair the damage when it occurs. And that the real trick to living a happy and free life is dodging the marketers and advertisers, you know?"

"Now that you put it that way…"

"I'm just saying we should be smarter than that. This absurdity is real, right? But it doesn't have to feel real."

As I drive, I attempt to wrap my low horsepower mind around Blakey's thoughts. Meanwhile, he coughs into his fist and leans his head back on the neck rest in his seat. "Is your wife still going forward with the divorce?"

I don't even bother fighting it. "I think so."

"That's too bad."

"I think she's seeing someone else."

"Really? How did you find that out?"

"I didn't find it out for sure. I just think so. Normal reasons. Being late, not answering her phone, running a lot of errands when she hates leaving the house."

"She's agoraphobic, right?"

"Yeah."

"She take pills for that?"

"Blakey, she takes a pill to eat, to sleep, to shit, for the bugs that live in her toenails, her non-watery eye, you name it."

"What are you going to do?"

"Not think about it is what I'm going to do. It's nice to be away from home and not have it thrown back in my face all the time."

"Sorry, didn't mean it like that."

"Okay. I know. I'm just saying. All that is waiting for me when I get back. I guess in a way I'm still back there, waiting for me too."

Chapter Five

WE EXIT ONTO 6th Street in Fayetteville. A frat boy eating onion rings and talking on his phone pulls out in front of me. When I honk, he does nothing. I honk again.

Blakey clears his throat. "Listen, Odom. I'm wondering if we can go see someone."

"Whose that, Blakey?"

"Never mind who. I'll show you where to go."

"What about my sister?"

"I'm waiting to hear back on her exact address. We'll get to her and that black boy. His name's Michael by the way. I forgot to tell you."

"I know his name, Blakey. Coached him before he skipped town."

"So let's go do this thing for me, okay?"

"Who is it?"

"A woman."

"Oh, no."

"It's not like that. I'll show you where to go."

Blakey points straight ahead, "Keep going through the light. You'll be taking a left up this way, past the high school. Look for Hill Street."

"Left on Hill Street?"

"I'll show you."

I turn on Hill Street and follow it through a tree-clogged neighborhood full of small, older homes and faded apartment buildings. Blakey tells me to look for a big white house on the left. When I see what I think is the house, I point at it and he nods his head. He tells me to park anywhere.

"How do you know if she's home?" I look around. There are a mix of cars up and down the street, mostly dented pickup trucks and even a few Hondas. I don't see a '97 though.

"She's always home."

"Who is this woman? And she lives in this big house?"

"It's actually four apartments inside."

Blakey gets out of the car before I can ask any more questions. He reaches for his breast pocket, lights up, surveys the street. I count the time in my head. When I get to thirteen seconds I ask him what he's doing.

"I'm going in," he says.

"Yeah, go in, Blakey. We got things to do."

"Right."

Two bleach-blonde sorority girls who look to be about twenty years old emerge from between the white house and another little house sitting behind it. They're smiling and carrying purses and backpacks. When they see me, they stop smiling and look down. Their pace quickens. Something is understood between the two of them. I watch them walk, trying to figure out what I missed.

"Quit staring at them girls, Odom," Blakey says.

"I'm not staring."

"You're scaring them."

"Why? I'm not doing anything. I thought you were going in."

"I am in fact going, and while I'm gone you should chew on this, and chew slowly: you're an old guy in a ten year old car. That's enough to scare most girls."

"I'm hardly old, Blakey."

"Try telling that to them," he says. They're already down on the other side of the street. I turn back to Blakey and he's walking up the grass to the house. I roll down the windows, rest my head back and wait. I feel sleepy and adjust my seat, pushing it back a little and stretch my legs out, folding my arms across my stomach. The air is cool; it's tinged with the smell of uncooked gasoline and lingering cigarette smoke. The breeze blows in short gusts, carrying the tainted air back into the car. I feel it across my face like someone is running their fingertips over my forehead, cheeks and lips. I move towards sleep. I find what I'm looking for and keep going, journeying past sleep where no one's fingers can find me.

I feel movement and open my eyes. A door slams in the distance. It's dark outside. Blakey is putting on his seat belt and popping a piece of nicotine gum in his mouth. I look over at him, waiting for him to say something, to explain what has happened—why it's dark and to assure me that I am who I think I am. I close my eyes again wanting to rejoin the secret place behind my eyes.

I watch Blakey put a new patch on his arm and toss the old one out the window.

"What are you doing, Blakey?"

"What do you mean?"

"You can't chew the gum and wear the patches while you're still smoking."

"Says who?"

"Never mind." I slide my seat back to its driving position and wipe my eyes. "What time is it?"

"I don't know," he says.

"Was it everything you thought it'd be?" I start the car up.

"I suppose so," he says. He mechanically works the gum in his mouth. He parks the wad of gum between his gum and lip like a tobacco dip and continues talking. "And to answer your next question, that's where my wife lives."

I look at the house, then Blakey.

"Your wife? You're not married. You divorced her, what's her name, twenty years ago."

"No, we're still married." He rolls his window up almost all the way. "Never got a divorce. I still care about her. We just can't live together."

"Huh? She was the one who had…"

"Our kid. Yeah."

I decide not to pry too much, but have to ask, "What happened?"

"You know, isn't that the biggest question in life. It's not where did we come from or what happens when we die or what's really out there in space. The biggest and most important question is exactly that, just two words—what happened. And the answer is always the same. No matter what, no matter where, the answer is always I don't know."

"You're right about that."

Although I indirectly agree to change the subject I seem to be unable to select a new topic for discussion. Instead we sit quietly. The air is filled with Blakey's chewing. Part of me is waiting for him to start talking again and go off on a tangent. Blakey has long been afflicted with this condition of his, this thinking-out -loud stuff he does, trying to make sense of things. He really thinks he has it figured out. Sometimes he does have something to say that is worth repeating. That's why I always listen.

His cell phone rings. The conversation is short and he folds the phone in half and jams it back into his pants pocket. He tells me the phone call was from one of his eagle eyes, who has produced the address to another house. Blakey won't actually tell me the address but shows me how to get there. After driving for just a few minutes he leans over and slaps his palm against the window, as if he were trying to crush an insect.

"What?"

"We just passed it."

"Where?" I hit the brakes.

"Gosh, darnit, Odom, keep driving, be cool."

I speed back up. "What do I do Blakey?"

"Just pull it over, right here is fine."

I do as I'm told and bring the car to an abrupt halt behind a school bus parked in front of a purple house. "Like this, Blakey? Is this good?" I say, as if I was talking to a three year-old.

"This will work."

"Thank god for that."

A bearded man who looks to be in his sixties leaves the purple house. He takes a bite from a granola bar and bends over to adjust his homemade leather sandals. He walks up to the school bus and climbs in. I expect the bus to start up, shooting white smoke from the tailpipes, but it doesn't. It just sits there.

Blakey gets out of the car and tells me to stay put. A car approaches, moving suspiciously slowly, the driver steering with one hand, and his other hand hanging out the window. He's wearing a red ball cap that is clearly too big for his head, most likely a souvenir buy at a small town gas station.

"Hey!" I shout from inside the car. "Blakey, that's a… that's your guy. The guy from inside the Paved Street Café. When we were in Louisiana. Look!"

"Where?"

The car rolls by and I get a good look at him. He smiles at me. I open my mouth to say something but I am frozen in the act. Then he raises his left arm which had been hanging over the side and gives me the middle finger. I look up at Blakey and his focus is off down the street, oblivious to the drama happening just ten feet from him. The car passes by and goes out the way we came in.

"Blakey! That is one of your guys. What's he doing here?"

"Who?"

"There, that car that just went by." I get out of the car and point the way the car went. I feel like one of those morons who's pointing to where they swear a UFO had landed and abducted them.

"I didn't see nothing," he says. "You're imagining things. Wait here."

I throw my hands in the air, dramatically, even though I know it means nothing.

"Look Odom. I'm the only representative from Blakey Flake's Intimate Resolutions in the State of Arkansas. Everyone else is down in Louisiana. Most aren't even working this case. There's no reason for them to be up here. This is a small fee job. This is mostly a favor for you."

"What do you mean small fee? I thought we're friends."

"We are friends. Friends get the small fee. And the friendlier you are, the better the savings. Keep that in mind."

"You're kidding me, right?"

"Relax. Sit down, take a deep breath. Call your wife and kid or something."

"That's not going to happen."

Blakey climbs back out of the car and lights up. "Sooner or later," he says. "Sooner or later."

There is this small issue with my son that is bothering me, aside from the fact that he's not really my kid, biologically speaking. It's not that he's asking too many questions—that's a good thing—but he's asking things I can't tell him yet. He wants to know about his grandfather and why we don't go to church the way everyone else does. Why we don't celebrate holidays. He wants to know why we do his schooling at home, why he doesn't play ball, why he doesn't have any friends. He's not old enough to understand what it means to be a Shiloh in Frothmouth, Arkansas—how the Shilohs have been key players in the development of this country of ours. The Shilohs founded this town about 200 years ago. The actual year is uncertain. No one seems to know for sure, which seems odd when I think about it. But there are stranger things in life. This at least has the rudiments of historical fact. The Shiloh's swept in from Tennessee, fleeing the march of the Baptist tent preachers; they built a school, a store, established a mayor's office. Even today though, it's still not listed on the map. That was their intent. It was a secret. You don't just drive by Frothmouth. You have to have a reason to find it.

It's because of all the knowledge we possessed about reality, how the world truly exists, that R.W.B., Inc. turned on us and tried to repair the "damage" we'd caused. They did it systematically. My daddy says that the money laundering wasn't the issue. But the Shiloh's did it right. We spread ourselves thin, across all kinds of businesses, enterprises, commercial ventures and so on; we had a hand in every pocket. At every board meeting, every congressional hearing, every Senate vote, there's a Shiloh lurking somewhere.

Then my daddy disappeared one day and it's been strangely quiet ever since.

Daddy always traveled. He drove hundreds of miles without thinking twice about it. He'd say he was driving to Atlanta and he'd be back the next night. Just like that, non-stop to Atlanta for a one hour meeting and back. He never flew. He distrusted machines in general, thought the government had their fingerprints all over them patents and rights and procedures—even if they didn't know he was sitting in row 12, seat A, they could find a way to figure out where he was. And who really knew where the pilot was headed. In a car, he could at least steer the wheel.

I would go with him on the shorter trips to places like Tulsa, Shreveport or Dallas or Kansas City. He'd write a note to Dr. Witten, our principal, and get me excused from school. To save time during the trip he'd listen to tapes. Self-empowerment tapes, with "coded messages" about the operation. "I'm preparing for the meeting," he would say, when I told him the tapes were boring. "It's important for you not to know anything. Just go to sleep." And I'd go to sleep, with the slight hint of burning oil through the car and the voice of some self-assured, Anglo baritone voice slipping into the distance.

Daddy went everywhere. He drove big cars—not hot rods or Cadillacs, but in-betweens, rusted out Delta 88s and used Grand Marquis with high odometer readings and botched paint jobs. And he dressed very unconventionally for a man in his position: tennis shoes with mismatched socks, jeans with cigarette burn-holes, t-shirts with every conceivable logo or saying, some with punk rock band insignias or advertisements for tow truck companies. This was a man who if you saw him you'd think he ran a cheap motel for a living, sitting all day at a crossword puzzle with a rackety metal fan blowing in his face. That was part of the pride I had in him, knowing he was anything but. Knowing he carried thick bundles of hundred dollar bills and phone numbers of people no one knew even existed. Daddy said that the folks who drove fancy cars and sported rings the size of Blow Pops were the world's new money; their wealth floating on the whims of Wall Street. The people who were really established were the ones who had to bury their wealth in the woods and pretend to be like everyone else.

I liked riding along with him. The only times we ever talked is when we were out in the woods or in the car. When it was just the two of us, rolling along the highway at two in the morning in the middle of Tennessee or Missouri, he'd tell me things. He'd say, "There's something you need to know." And that's how it always started and I knew then that he was passing along something of great importance. My daddy would tell me that in revealing certain things I would be included in a small minority, maybe a half dozen people, who knew what he was about to tell me. And then there were the things only he and I were to know about.

It was during these drives that I learned the details about many of the operations and moneymaking schemes the Shiloh Foundation had undertaken. One of the most prominent and easiest was hooking up with promising televangelists and "managing" their careers, thus, siphoning a large percentage of their tax-free profits into our accounts. He had his own television show in the South for a while. It wasn't him that was on the show but rather a guy named Don Duggar, who spoke the Lord's word and sang his spirit three times a week in twenty-four markets from North Carolina to Texas. The Don Duggar Show ran in the 1970s and was created and produced by none other than my father. It was pure profit. That money is still around. But there's still a mystery surrounding that entire escapade as well. Don Duggar went off the air in 1977 and has never been heard from again. I think the official line was that as the disco revolution began sweeping the nation Duggar was dragged into a life of sin. The unofficial line is that he was invited to Kansas City and given a job interview for a "higher" position. No one knows whether that higher position was based in this world, or the next.

A lot of the Shiloh Foundation dealings were church-related. It's so easy to sucker most people when you're hiding behind a facade of Christian righteousness. Another common tactic was to set up illegitimate home repair, roofing, landscape, concrete companies long enough to lure in clients and take their money, before running off. Some of the crews my father oversaw adopted similar techniques that the Irish Travelers over in South Carolina used. Knocking on doors, offering home repair work, taking the deposits or 50% payment, work a few days and then leave. Or setting up fake falls and seeking damages from companies. All of it.

We ran a small chain of payday lender outfits. The Shilohs founded a trucking company they later sold for a huge profit. They started hauling pulp dust from the sawmills in southeast Arkansas and drove them up to northwest Arkansas where they sold it to chicken farmers who used the pulp dust for the cages. I forgot what the scam was exactly but I know it ended with the FDA declaring all chickens in that part of the U.S. "unfit for human consumption."

All my life people have whispered to me, when no one was standing nearby, that my father was bona fide crazy. Mayor Ferguson, even before he was mayor, would sometimes pull me out of the Sunday soul food serving-line and ask if things were all right at home. People outside Garner's Gas & Snack would give me strange looks. They'd make comments about how they seen my daddy walking naked down the road holding an empty Hefty garbage bag up to the wind, or something like that. When I'd get angry and ask them to repeat what they'd said they'd look away. I've waved my fists many a time at these folks. When I get real angry I get this look, people tell me. It makes them quiet and wish they'd never said anything.

This campaign to discredit my father's reputation and role has been running for as long as I can remember. Bree asks me why Sparkman can't interact with the community at large. Well, that's one reason.

There's not much left to our enterprise: me, a half-deaf half-brother, an uncle and some second cousins I've lost track of. I have no idea how the Red, White and Blue, Inc. found this town but I guess they did, and when they did they dismantled almost everything. It was dubbed Operation Condor in the newspapers; they sent nineteen Foundation Members to prison. A few disappeared forever into the witness protection program. Donned fake moustaches and took up residence in a Yankee state.

We don't do much anymore. At least I don't. I really try and stay away from it all. I've never been one these people I'm supposed to be. A crook. A conman. An oyster.

Blakey knows I'm sterile when it comes to this life of crime. Hell, Blakey's the criminal kind. He don't care much about what happens any farther than what he can see on a clear day. He says that's how he stays sane. Says that people who talk like they care really don't. I admit to being an optimist; Blakey himself will tell you he's as pessimistic as they come. And naturally I think I'm inclined to gain the most rewards and victories. But Blakey seems to lose the least and gain the least at the same time. It works well for him. I've heard him say on many occasions to aim high, expect low and live a more fulfilling life.

Blakey used to work for my daddy. That's how I know him. We go way back. Years ago Blakey had taken a summer job in between his semesters at Louisiana State University working for Shiloh Concessions, a company that ran soda and snack stands at concerts, fairs, and festivals. The thing was, we got our soda and snacks for free. We stole them off of the Louisiana dockyards and bought the dockyard accountant a new convertible. Shiloh Concessions was run by a guy named Portis Hays down in Alexandria, Louisiana. Portis and the boys took an immediate liking to Blakey. Thought he was about as smart as a kid could hope to be, although you wouldn't think he could point to an ocean on a world map by the looks of him, almost bald already and always smoking cigarettes and mumbling to himself some grand idea he'd cooked up from some book he'd just read. Still, he would always come up with more money in the till than we expected.

So they started to "test" Blakey. They had their ways to evaluate potential partners. After many months Blakey was officially invited in. There is a lengthy ceremony full of rituals and sworn allegiance and secrecy. The final ceremony, I am told, takes place in the woods. They accuse you of something and show you a rope in the trees and then hand you a shovel and tell you to dig. Once you've dug good and deep they tell you to give the shovel back to them. They turn you around until you're looking at the hole; you never see the shovel when it hits the back of your head. You wake up in a motel room with an envelope on the table. Inside the envelope is a piece of paper explaining everything you need to know. He is still "in" even today, although he is no longer active. You're always "in." You never get out. If you want to go inactive it's a process, and it often ends with another rope and metal striking your head. They call it "turnover." But even inactives like Blakey, even if they storm motel rooms and help the cops to make a living, are still tied to the Shiloh Foundation. That's why we're friends, and why in a lot of ways he is where he is today. And why, for example, he didn't go to prison after that stunt he pulled in Shreveport. For all his smarts and graduate degrees he's still naïve enough to believe that his courtroom art lesson was what kept him from getting used as currency in jail. He doesn't know how many jury members drove away in convertibles once the verdict had been handed down.

Blakey did some of the highest order jobs for the Shilohs. In the line of work he did, burnout is common, turnover is high and most don't ever get very far in the actual training, far enough to actually do a job. But Blakey did. It was business. By the time he was twenty-five he was retired from Shiloh. He went back to Baton Rouge, finished his bachelor's degree and then took a suitcase of money straight to Tulane, presented it to the dean of graduate admissions. Shortly after that he opened another suitcase, and got himself a teaching job there at Tulane as a guest lecturer. After one semester he bailed and wandered around a bit, through Louisiana and East Texas, working on oil rigs and staying out of trouble. But trouble found him in the form of sex; after six months he tried to beat it in the dead of night but got tracked down himself and shown a surprise of his own: a little baby boy. The woman proclaimed it to be "marrying time" and that's what Blakey did. He hauled her and the kid back to Louisiana and began teaching art appreciation at Middle Louisiana Community College in Alexandria. This woman of his, Luanne was her name, had bigger aspirations than being married to a community college instructor. "You get paid shit. And you talk shit. If you add that up it equals shit," she'd yell at him.

Blakey says Luanne liked to stay good and drunk most of the time.

Luanne had family up in St. Joseph, Missouri, and she told Blakey that's where they were going. She was tired of Louisiana and every other state it bordered with. Blakey said he wasn't moving anywhere. Luanne planned on staying up there long enough to save up money for one of them one-room efficiencies in Hollywood, California. She was going to be an actress of some type. Their little boy died when he was two years old. He had some rare heart ailment that made it stop beating in the middle of the night. His name was Daniel.

That's when everything went haywire for Blakey and Luanne. I think that's why they're still close, even all these years later. However unexpected, the two of them, together, once created something beautiful.

Chapter Six

WE KNOCK AT THE DOOR to Margaret Kenzer's house and then we knock some more. We can hear people walking around, dropping things, slamming doors. I look at Blakey. "Knock again," he says. "We don't have warrants. All we can do is knock. And we'll knock all day if we have to. I've done it before, one time..."

"I got it, Blakey. We're knocking. Your turn. My knuckles are starting to bruise."

The door opens. A red-haired guy in a Superman robe balances a glass of clear liquid between his thumb and forefinger. His eyes look up at us and then back down.

"She's not here, man. When are you guys going to quit coming around?"

"Is Margaret here?" Blakey shouts over his shoulder, ignoring Superman's greeting.

"Margie!" he yells. "Margie, it's for you again."

"Who is it?" a woman yells.

"I think it's the police again, Margie. I can't tell." He looks up at us again. "There are four of them this time. I think we're in some serious shit."

I glance at Superman. "Must be some kryptonite in that glass."

He just stands in the doorway, swaying back and forth.

From down the hallway comes a woman. She is walking fast and is noticeably steadier than our doorman.

"What?" she says. "No, let me guess. You're looking for Birdshit. Well, she isn't here. She was here. But she's not anymore. Come on in, take a look around, you won't be the first ones and probably not the last." She pokes her head outside a bit and searches the street.

"We aren't the first ones?" Blakey says.

"Thank you for your time," I say and begin to walk away.

"No, some guy in a big red ball cap just came by looking for her and before him two other guys."

"Did they say what for?" Blakey says.

"No, just wanted to know where she was. I told them what I knew."

"And that is?"

"That she and that boyfriend of hers are on their way up to Kansas City."

"Kansas City?"

"Did I say it wrong? Yes, Kansas City."

I raise my hand. "Did you say a red ball cap?"

"Yes, a red one. I told Birdshit I would tell y'all she was heading to Tulsa and get y'all going the wrong way. But I am not going to lie to law enforcement, no way. I got things in this house that could put me away for years, so no point in lying about anything now." Her eyes are pinned to a stain on the carpet. She fidgets and walks in place, picking up her feet one at a time. Her energy level increases. Her talking speeds up, gets louder. As if the last few minutes hadn't even happened, she shifts topic, starts to talk about shoelaces, the planet Jupiter and numbers. I listen. Blakey nods politely as he lights a cigarette. He feigns an impatient interest.

"…because I was born in 1971 and if you add that up it equals eighteen which is how old I was when I was first arrested and I spent two years on probation, subtract two and that is sixteen, the age I was when I first started shooting speed and I paid ten bucks for my first bag, ten plus 1971 is 1981, the year my little sister was born…."

It all made sense. It always added up. We walked away before she finished. From the distance we heard her continue. She was on a roll. I almost ask Blakey who Margaret Kenzer is, and why we came here. Then I decide it's pointless.

"That son of a bitch," Blakey says.

"What's that?"

"The red ball cap guy. You were right. He was here."

"Who is he?"

"Mateo Panadero."

"Does he always wear a red ball cap?"

"I don't know. Maybe. Why?"

"I don't know. That cap just pisses me off. Something about it."

Back in the car, Blakey says he's not going up to Kansas City.

"Fayetteville is as far north as I go. I'm no Yankee. I belong down here."

We understand that Birdshit is probably hauling it to Kansas City and hoping Uncle Lou will take over from there. What we can't figure out is why this Mateo Panadero cat and the others are onto them.

"Blakey you don't want to go to Kansas City because when you were up there before, we all went out to eat at an Italian restaurant and when the waiter explained to you that the chicken was sautéed and served in extra virgin olive oil, you said you didn't want extra olive oil, just the normal amount. Everyone in the entire restaurant heard you."

"That's reason enough for a man to no longer care for a place. Besides, that's not why I don't want to go."

"Then why?"

"Well, your deaf brother, for one. That kid is plain odd as a three-sided nickel."

"Gavin? He's not deaf. He's only deaf in one ear."

"Deaf enough to say about half his words wrong. When Gavin was a kid I remember one time the little turd was running around screaming about how the Tall Guy was on TV. It was his favorite show."

"The Tall Guy?"

"The Lee Majors show. Only thing is, it was called "The Fall Guy," not the Tall Guy."

"Does it really freak you out that much, that he mispronounced the name of a television show twenty-five years ago? You buy cigarettes from people who speak in one language and think in another."

"Don't we all."

It is true that my half-brother, or more accurately, the byproduct of one of my daddy's infidelities is partially deaf, 55% deaf to be exact. When you say something to him you have about a 45% chance of him understanding you. He won't wear hearing aids either. Tried it a few times, said the real world is too noisy for him. He prefers his world, says it's a lot quieter. This is something that I can only think I understand.

Understand or not, he's a Shiloh and that's where the nitpicking stops in my book. He works at Uncle Lou's restaurant. He's got big dreams, always has. His grand aspiration is to be a documentary filmmaker. He's been working on this one project now for about three years. It's a Where Are They Now type of deal that involves tracking down heavy metal rock stars from the 1980s. And what I really mean is that he tracks down the no-name bands. More specifically, he's been trying to find participants in Penelope Spheeris' 1988 *Decline of Western Civilization: The Metal Years* documentary. It's a Where Are They Now documentary about people who appeared in a different documentary.

The Spheeris documentary featured up-and-coming hopefuls and other burnouts in the Los Angeles hair-band scene around the year of 1987 or 1988. Most of the interviews follow industry standards: sex, drugs, rock n' roll, I'll die trying to make it and if I don't make it, dig me a grave and give me a rope to hang myself—romantic dreamer sound bytes. I think Gavin wanted to see if any of them followed through on their threat—to commit suicide if they didn't make it. Turns out, most of the bands that appeared in the documentary didn't garner any notoriety, fame or accolades whatsoever. Most couldn't even muster the required courage to kill themselves. So where are they now? What are they doing? Of all the things Gavin could be doing with his life, he's scraping through skid row, looking at each piece of white trash like it might hold the answer to tinseltown fame. I don't see how anyone with objectives as harmless as this can trigger the opprobrium of someone like Blakey. But there are a lot of things I know I don't understand.

Blakey isn't finished with Kansas City. "I ain't going. I don't do well up there. Everyone talks to me like I'm retarded. Hell, I ain't retarded, I got a graduate degree and I've been a subscriber to *Harper's* for ten years. They don't understand what a Southern man values. I don't belong up there. I hardly belong here in Fayetteville, with all these phony baloney frat boys I used to fail out of my class at Tulane. This is as far north as I go, right here." He slaps the window with his palm. "So you can drop me off back at that white house we were at earlier, and pick me up on your way back down if you'd like."

"I'm not leaving you here with Superman and Space-Woman. I need you, your expertise, and your instincts."

Blakey huffs a little, then folds up his shirt-sleeve. He pulls off his nicotine patch in a slow-peel-it's-going-to-hurt-at-any-moment manner, but I can tell it isn't really hurting him. He attempts to throw it out the window. Instead of going airborne the breeze knocks it down; it drops into that little space between the seat and the door where the food crumbs live forever, free from the reaches of vacuum hoses.

"Oh, crap," he says.

"Leave it," I say. I'd given up caring for my car years ago. Its gradual demise is as natural as aging. Why fight it. Life gets shorter every day. "Why are you even still wearing those things?"

"Because you bought them for me. It'd be rude not to give 'em a try."

"But you're not trying."

"I am too trying. Will you pull down your visor? I think there's a pack up there."

I drop my sun visor and pull out a pack of Nuggets. I think they've used up all the possible names for cigarettes.

Blakey pulls one out and says, "Before we get on the highway, I need you to pull over so I can buy a few packs for the road."

"So you're going?"

"Yeah, yeah. I'll go. But seriously, pull over and let me buy another pack."

"It's not even a four hour drive, how many packs you need?"

"Don't hassle me. Just don't," Blakey mumbles, a fresh cigarette hanging out of the corner of his mouth. He digs his green lighter out of his front pocket, cranks out a flame and leans the tip of the cigarette over the dancing light, inhales a sweeping rush of relief and then violently coughs out the first drag. The coughing subsides momentarily; he takes advantage of his good health and quickly drags another three-second pull. This one he manages to keep trapped in his lungs long enough for a glint of pleasure to polish the outsides of his eyes; as he passively lets the smoke fall out of his lungs, he begins to cough again, loudly and hard. When he stops he says, "Damn, I must be getting sick or something."

"You're not getting sick. You're coughing."

"That's a hell of a cough."

"Smoke away, Blakey. Smoke away. See if I care."

Chapter Seven

BLAKEY BUYS NUGGETS from another Arab. If and when the conservative press' predictions come true and there is an uprising amongst the invisible-handed infidels, our nicotine addicts will be the first in our ranks to fall. The bridges their cigarette taxes built will fall next.

There's not much to look at driving north on U.S. 71, through the southwest corner of Missouri. Back when I first started driving up this way it was a rural route, coming to a complete stop at several places, requiring a right- or left-hand turn to stay on 71. Nowadays they've built a bypass that goes around the metropolis of Joplin; they're adding lanes, widening existing ones, and the entire southwest corridor glows with strip centers full of chain stores and gas stations that sell Ozark souvenirs, fountain drinks and whiskey. The largest retailer in the universe is allegedly headquartered in Bentonville, Arkansas not far from the Missouri state line. But that HQ is all window dressing. On the Missouri side is where the underground data mining takes place, all the billions of transactions and dollar amounts and personal information is stored, sifted, analyzed, grouped, arranged, labeled, copied, stored again and sold off to the highest bidder. They say that if you shop often enough, Wal-Mart will predict your buying habits and will literally restock a can of chicken noodle soup on the shelf in anticipation of your buying that same can of soup in three weeks. Blakey says them's fighting words for the whole determinism versus free will debate. The invisible hand. Cartesian graphs. I tell him I'm not all that familiar. He says not to worry; people like me don't need to worry about it.

I tell Blakey we're driving over underground bunkers full of the fastest computers in the world. He listens and slowly nods, like he does when something's really sticking. He doesn't say anything. I think that's because it took him ten minutes to get his cough under control and I don't think he feels much like talking, probably afraid it may lead to another spell. But he still lights a cigarette every fifteen minutes, rolling the passenger side power window down a third of the way, sending a golden shower of sparks down floating behind us into the darkness. Whatever conversation we'd struck up was drowned in the uproarious Missouri wind.

I can't help but see the similarities in the Shiloh Foundation and Wal-Mart. The enormous power they've amassed. Their secretive business operations. Still. They're like the carnival barkers that we used to employ through Shiloh Concessions, who we'd tell to act dumb when they got caught cheating. When of course we knew full well they were trying to cheat at every possible opportunity. Wal-Mart's no different. They're nothing more than carnies hawking cheap crap and doing everything they can to make you feel good about buying it, more and more of it. They intimidate, harass and threaten, then play dumb when they're caught. Send complaints to them professional window dressers in Arkansas; forget about that bunker buried across state lines. It's the model for success in America. It is what it is, as Uncle Lou used to say. Big yellow smiles stuck to everything. I think the best thing Shiloh could've ever done was to crush Sam Walton when we had the chance.

"When I was a kid," I tell Blakey, who is lighting another Nugget, consumed by the Missouri roar. Anyhow, when I was a kid, we spent a lot of summers in Kansas City. Back then we had more family and friends living there. Nowadays, like I've said, it's really only Uncle Lou up there and a few others. In those days there was Uncle Vilonia too. He was a real estate agent, among other things; sold "retirement" homes to the Chicago mob guys back in the 1970s. My daddy said I'd ride along sometimes with Uncle Vilonia and listen to him sell houses. Sometimes one of the mob guys would ask me to go fetch their cigarettes from the dash in their cars. The guys would tip me a five-dollar bill for the job. They got a kick out of watching my reaction to the five-dollar bill. I always refused; I had good manners. They'd say, "Ah, kid, take the money," and then give me a pat on the head. I don't remember any of these stories, personally. Apparently they ended abruptly. No one knows what happened to Uncle V. He's been gone for a while. We don't imagine he'll be coming back from wherever he went. Some say that someone from the inside had to take Vilonia on a long walk. That's how we talk in the family. Why don't you go take him for a walk. A long walk in the woods. Nature calls. The nature of the business. You get the idea. Uncle V got caught up in the wrong things for the wrong reasons. It was no secret what he did, paid no taxes, made gobs of money, was a Shiloh and had intimate connections with all the major Midwest mob organizations. He was even bold enough to go on the Don Duggar Show and made a personal plea for donations to save the starving children in Africa. A Sally Struthers when the real Sally Struthers was still on *All in the Family*. A loud mouth. That's what my daddy called him. Who knows? Maybe Red, White and Blue, Inc. gave him a fake moustache, a glue stick, and a rent-controlled apartment in Philadelphia. Maybe he's watching daytime TV right now. No way to know for sure. As far as I'm concerned, he's gone.

"Blakey, you remember Uncle V?"

"Nothing more than you know." He lights a cigarette, coughs and looks outside again.

Yeah, so he's gone and, of course, he's dead—but no one talks like that. He's gone. In one way or another he's really dead. Funny, isn't it? Can you imagine being dead and no one knowing for sure if you are or not. Or people won't even acknowledge that you're dead. No headstone, no ashes, no ceremony, no obituary in the papers, everything you've ever owned given away, thrown away or set on fire. Like you didn't even exist. Just a memory, for a little while. And when you're no longer a memory—no one alive remembers you—you become history. And we all know that no one pays attention to history.

But to be clear we never mingled too much with the real Mafiosos. Daddy Shiloh didn't want things that way. They did their thing. We did ours. It was understood and left at that. When the two paths got crossed, as in Uncle V's case, well, it wasn't good for Uncle V. And the mob guys found a new real estate agent and life went on for everyone. Another day is always the start of something new. Right?

And here's something you probably didn't know. Blakey, back in the old days, took guys on walks. The long nature walks. That was his job.

Chapter Eight

BIRDSHIT SHILOH AND UNCLE VILONIA have one thing in common: neither has ever married. That itself is enough mystery to last most folks a lifetime. Birdshit's never been like everyone else, always enjoyed doing her own things, never finding much joy in rock music or drinking keg beer with boys in parking lots. She goes in for the stiff stuff, the hard stuff. Whiskey and water. Lies on our faded red couch, fingering invisible piano keys. Goes on long walks through town. Always existed on the margins of things, like an ornament everyone liked to look at and talk about. Like I've said her looks have been reason enough for men to drive from as far away as Fort Smith and Magnolia and even over from Tupelo, Mississippi just to take a look at her. Most propose marriage on the spot—Momma hiding around the corner of our long hallway, sparkling with pride. Birdshit standing behind a screen door that doesn't shut all the way, "Thank you for your proposal, um, what's your name again, but I'm afraid I'm going to have to refuse." Birdshit wasn't too big on reasons. Some would come back in fancy cars, foreign-tailored suits, sporting engagement rings the size of Blow Pops. Hell, former Arkansas governor Jim Guy Tucker and Wal-Mart henchman David Glass made their very own personal appeals. Some even say Clinton himself sent an unnamed accomplice to the house on his behalf requesting a private night of torrid entanglements. As far as I know, he did not have sexual relations with my sister.

As Birdshit sent them away one by one, Momma would cry herself to sleep.

The thing is, Momma doesn't need to work and despite the fact that our screen door doesn't shut all the way—never has—she still lives in one of the nicer houses in Frothmouth: four bedrooms, two and a half baths, landscaped yard that she doesn't have to touch, screened in back porch with sixty acres surrounding, part meadow, part woods. That's being a Shiloh for you.

So what do Momma and Birdshit do all day, with no men or kids or 9-to-5's?

They've fallen hard for daytime talk shows full of gossip, for crap magazines full of pictures of celebrities getting in and out of vehicles. Birdshit says she still plays the piano from time to time and works on her poems, but other than that I don't really know.

She dated a few boys—the ones that didn't propose to her or go all crazy when they saw her. Ass grabbing, winking and whistling types were not Birdshit's favored potential mates. She and Mayor Ferguson used to debate the meaning of courtship over soul food. She said a diamond is just another type of whistling; and boys that whistled came a dime a dozen. But there were a few boys. The one I remember most was a left-handed flutist who played with her in the Little Rock Symphony. His name was Beck, like the German beer. When I said this he blinked. I don't think he'd ever had a German beer. Birdshit and Beck dated for seven months. He always seemed embarrassed to be out in public with her. She was so naturally alluring and he was so oddly repulsive, with post-traumatic acne scars littering his face and neck and a stature that was slightly bent forward. He was frail and had long bony fingers and a big mess of black hair that was always wet for some reason, as if he ran water through it obsessively, like a woman might.

Beck took off for the Pittsburgh Symphony as soon as a flute position opened up. The most bizarre piece of this puzzle was that Beck left town and never called, wrote or acknowledged her ever again. Poor Birdshit didn't leave her bedroom for three months. She even went out and bought a cheap flute and taught herself how to play; no doubt playing the same melodies that Beck had first wooed her with. After she'd mastered the flute, playing note for note along with her James Galway tapes, she broke it in half and never played it again.

As much as Momma wants her out of the house, it's been my duty to keep her there. She doesn't do well on her own. She lived by herself once right after the breakup with Beck. She was determined to stand on her own and prove herself. That lasted five weeks before I had to go pick her up from her Little Rock apartment complex and drive her back to Frothmouth, defeated and crying the whole way, balled up in the back seat. "I can't do it," she said over and over again.

"I don't know why I can't do it. I'm so scared. Everything terrifies me."

Doctors in Memphis and Little Rock have put her on a long list of medications to help better her chances of being able to cope. The good days have been few. What she needs is to stay with Momma as long as she can. She causes problems sometimes and runs her mouth a little too. She talks about Daddy in a bad kind of way that doesn't need to be repeated. Sometimes when she's not careful she hints at things that we agreed a long time ago not to talk about.

The first time Birdshit had one of her "episodes" was around the time Daddy disappeared.

Her life since then has been a series of "episodes." We all thought her brilliance in some areas compensated for her under-development in others. Yet great piano playing didn't make up for her lack of ability to function on a day-to-day basis. All of the doctors seemed to agree that some biochemical confusion was occurring. Although all blood tests, brain scans, CT's, EEGs, EKGs, etc., revealed no abnormalities. This seemed to point to some kind of psychological trauma or scarring. One doctor, a Minnesotan in West Helena was convinced that Birdshit was making everything up. That it was all in her head.

So since everything was in her head, the Minnesotan referred her to a psychologist in Pine Bluff, Dr. Elleridge, a tall black man with a snow-white beard. He asked her a lot of questions and made her take home a test with even more questions, the MMPI—Minnesota Multiphasic Personality Inventory. We thought it was strange that Dr. Elleridge was the one who gave it to her since he was from Arkansas and the Minnesotan, for whom the test was named after, had not been the one to administer it. Nonetheless, she plowed through the thousands of questions. It might not have been that many but it was a lot. I helped her with some of it, taking over when she was too exhausted to continue and did my best to answer the questions as I thought she would've answered them.

The test yielded nothing more than confirmation that her mind was fragmented. Dr. Elleridge thought there was a biochemical basis to this psychological disorganization. This meant she needed to see someone who could give her medicine. A psychiatrist. This doctor, the first of several psychiatrists, was Dr. Joanne Andler, who practiced in downtown Little Rock. She never asked Birdshit anything other than, "How are you feeling?" And my sister never said anything more than, "Fine." Dr. Andler wrote out a new prescription every few months. "Try this one," she'd say. My sister would sometimes ask, "But what if it doesn't work?" "We got plenty more to choose from," was the answer.

I couldn't make head or tail of the meds. I could barely pronounce the names of the active ingredients. But Birdshit sure could. On the meds, she would easily fall into a deep depression or just as quickly become agitated and violent, thrashing about, swinging her arms around and around as if she were performing some crazy ceremonial jig. Momma and I usually got elbows and arms smacking against our faces and rib cages when we tried to intervene. She used to cut herself too. Not like her suicide heroes, but cutting all the same. If you look closely, you can see the scars on her shins and forearms. Sometimes she'd get hooked on something and she wouldn't be able to stop it. Sometimes it was a word or a phrase; she once sent me a ream of paper with the phrase "the moon is a bastard seed" typewritten on it, like in *The Shining*. Sometimes it was a particular food or beverage. She'd eat nothing but hot dogs with no bun for three months straight. Or drink Dr. Pepper and nothing else for two weeks. One time she got on a red licorice kick that ended after only four days with a climactic gastrointestinal upheaval all over Momma's dining room carpet. The stain is still there, kind of like the screen door. The house is full of broken things, blemishes, things we could easily pay someone to repair but we—Momma and I—just don't get around to it. Either that or we have just accepted them.

Birdshit used to write me letters, long letters describing her innermost feelings about Beck. She wrote with both hands down opposite sides of a single page, her left hand scribbling melancholy tales of woe, her right stylistically more upbeat and promising, full of high expectations and goal-setting. She wrote poetry, lots and lots and lots of it. At times my mailbox would be overstuffed with yellow envelopes of her poems—each envelope crammed with so many pages that the metal clasp had broken off and she had to tape it shut. She wanted my feedback. Was she a poet? Tell me, she'd write. Tell me my fate. Thy a poet or thy not? She used words like "thy" as if they were going out of style now, instead of a few hundred years beforehand. I read each and every poem. Some were later published in a slim volume by Water Dribble Press, a small outfit in Little Rock. It was called *Alone And Lost At Sea.* There were a few reviews and brief mentions in regional literary magazines. I drove her to a few readings full of white-haired women and men with carefully trimmed beards. Unfortunately, her poetry celebrity soon vanished. That was years ago. All the same, everyone in Frothmouth, including myself has been awaiting her second volume for which a title has already been given: *Still Lost.*

The title poem, *Alone And Lost At Sea,* from her first volume: I memorized it.

No one knows what its like to be me:
A woman, alone and lost at sea.
No one to talk to or to hear from me
No one to soothe my cries of agony
No one to fear the future
And run from tomorrow
No one to comfort me
Or my sorrow.
No one knows what its like to be me:
A woman, alone and lost at sea.

Frothmouth doesn't have much history in fostering artistic types. So for whatever most of us couldn't understand about what she wrote and why she did, we knew that in some way it was something farther reaching than what we did from day to day.

I had long ago acknowledged Birdshit's poetic soul, as she called it. And frankly, I figured she'd be a suicide by now, like all her poetry heroes. Suicide heroes. Maybe that's why she had to take off.

I could go on and on. People like her do things and act in ways that supply thousands of stories. Her latest kick, although she calls it a hobby, is collecting useless crap. She's got a computer and a super fast internet connection that allows her to make multiple purchases instantaneously. And she does. She likes the online auctions and cheap crap-for-sale websites. She buys strands of hair that supposedly belonged to famous people, rare and valuable comic books, CDs, doll clothes, cooking utensils, and has about a dozen boxes of KaBoom! Spray Cleaner in her closet. I've seen the bills; Momma shows me. Momma refuses to pay her credit card bills so Birdshit just ignores the monthly statements and Momma collects them all and puts them in Birdshit's desk drawer. As of right now she owes an approximate total of $27,000. Momma has tried taking her computer away but Birdshit just got online at the library and ordered a new one. We're hoping it'll be a passing phase.

Birdshit isn't too worried about her credit score. She likes to say that she's surprised she's made it this far along. And when you ask her to explain what she means, she says, "That I'm alive. I thought I'd be dead by now."

There's a recurring dream she has that takes place in the woods behind our house. She's obsessed with murder and thinks that she will be murdered someday. Not that she believes there are people actively after her, she just thinks that she's already seen her death—that in a dream she was murdered—near a small body of water, a pond, or a man-made lake. She was murdered with a gun. A shotgun. I asked her once what did it feel like and if she died immediately or if she continued to live for a brief moment before she died.

She said that the impact is painless and likened it to being shoved or playfully pushed. Then, she says, the first thing you notice is an odd numbness and wetness. Blood. The blood is the first thing you *feel* once your brain figures out that something is seriously wrong. You look down, or *she* looks down in this dream, and sees the primary impact area in her lower-mid abdomen. It's noticeably caved in but it still doesn't feel like it's real. You're waiting for the punch line, to be let in on the joke, the trick. That lasts only for a second or two before the horror sets in. The horror isn't a terrified scream or panic, it's the realization that reality has shifted gears; your path has been severely altered; it's not just the fact that you're possibly bleeding to death and parts of your entrails and organs are visible, but that in no rational universe should this be actually happening. And of course, you're thinking, no shit this isn't supposed to be happening but it is. It's all brand new to you in a way that you'd never been required to imagine. And after this is Birdshit's favorite part: a blurry cognition, a realization that *I'm dying.* That unless something changes within the very next twenty or thirty seconds, you're dying. But the best part is that it isn't scary. A little sad, a delicate melancholy, but nothing more than being the last person to leave a movie theater after a sad movie, a sad love story to be more exact. Then you die. At the moment of death you feel a release, she says. You consciously notice it for a split second, maybe two or three at the most, that something is splitting you from your body, then that's it. You're dead.

Where are the bright lights, I asked. There are none. She says the bright light theory is something she thinks people have exaggerated because, she says, there is bright lighting around the periphery of your visual field as you're going through these stages and it's comforting but it isn't an essential light, it's not all there is, the way people make it out to be. There is no important essence in this light; it is just a feature of the experience.

And who murders you, and why? I asked.

I don't know, she says. And I'm glad I don't.

So you can see why this finding Birdshit is so important and why I had to get Blakey involved. I don't need her out on her own and don't need her going up to Kansas City and causing havoc on the little bit of family we have up there. They don't need to be bothered with it.

I can't say I've served as much of an example. Been married two times. The first was for three years to a girl from Gurnee, Illinois. We lasted about as long as you can on promises. Then the questions started. Mona liked to ask me if I thought space and time had a beginning or if the speed of light impressed me in any way. She wasn't about having kids. She wanted to have a career first. I said, "Why the hell you marry me for?" I promised to support her, she promised to have a kid. Neither of us really wanted to follow through with our end of the bargain. The last I saw her, she was driving off out of Frothmouth, declaring once and for all our marriage a failure. I didn't even bother to walk her to the car or peer out the window at her as she drove away. If I remember correctly I grabbed the latest *Sports Illustrated* swimsuit issue and sat on the toilet for half an hour. And when I was done I cautiously called her name out, "Mona? Mona?" for fear that she might have returned. But she hadn't, and didn't. I was safe. It was over.

My wife nowadays is a girl named Brianna, or Bree, fourteen years younger than I am; if all girls have a pretty card with a spending limit pre-approved by God, hers would be Platinum. Unfortunately, she's burned her balance on trinkets, spurious lovers, demands for toenail polish and Wal-Mart shopping sprees. And she picked up her own baggage: that kid, Sparkman, I was telling Blakey about. She gets a lot of looks from the proverbial parking lot kegger crowd and frankly it was those kinds of looks that got me noticing her in the first place. Amazing what a woman can gain in this world just from genetics. She can be real sweet too, when she wants to be. Not the brightest, which is fine by me; I learned my lesson from wife number one.

I think I really like Brianna because she doesn't ask too many questions about my daddy or what my family does or why whenever I quit a job I don't sweat it. Why sometimes I sit on the couch for days on end staring out the window or go a week without uttering a single word. Mona picked up on those things; she knew there was something I wasn't telling her. I promised to tell her. But I never did.

Bree, like me, doesn't do much. The thrust of her daily activities revolves around Sparkman and the ringing of her cell phone. A world I've been pretty much shut out of for the last year. She gets a call, she takes a prescription pill from the medicine cabinet, leaves. Words between us are rare. I imagine the homeschooling is going okay. Bree gives Sparkman workbooks to fill out and she checks the answers in her Teacher's Edition and then tells him his score. If he has a question or is confused about something she just repeats the answer from the Teacher's Edition. I'm a little skeptical of how much he retains. Then again, he's made the Dean's List and Honor Roll every semester since he began homeschooling.

One thing homeschooled kids don't have is their own football team. That's my biggest concern. Football, in my opinion, is even more important than some of the subjects they teach nowadays. Even Frothmouth High, student enrollment 89, has a varsity football team. The Shiloh Foundation insisted on it. We've funded the team for years. David Garner, heir to Garner's Gas & Snack, used to be the coach for awhile. His drinking got in the way of his play-calling, though. Sometimes the team would just line up with no play because David had fallen down drunk next to the orange Gatorade coolers and the quarterback would say hike and just stand there because he didn't know what to do.

The last time we won a game was in 1986 and that was only because of a scheduling mishap. We arrived at the field only to find out we were playing the Arkansas School for the Blind. We pulled out a victory even though they managed to score 14 points on us and recovered one fumble and intercepted two passes. They almost scored 21 points but Evan "The Bat" Fielder ran one of the intercepted passes into the wrong end zone. Still, we practice every day. As Assistant to the Assistant Football Coach, I can see determination in those kids' eyes. No matter how many times they trip in the tires and fall down, they're up like lightning when I toot the whistle.

Football aside, Spark is an okay kid. He reminds me a lot of my own daddy even though he ain't blood kin. Sparkman's also linked to his landscape: he's named for the town where Bree is from, another small Arkansas town, close to Arkadelphia. Kind of looks like Daddy, too, same blue eyes and tiny teeth. Their personalities match. They're the type whose thoughts you can never pin down. They can surprise you. Or you won't think they're paying attention, but they really are.

Birdshit used to come over and give Spark piano lessons. We have a piano in our house but Spark quit wanting to learn a few years ago. He complained that Birdshit was being hard on him. Birdshit had bought some beginner's level piano books at the big piano shop on Main Street in downtown Little Rock; she expected results. She was a concert pianist with a symphony, after all. But Spark just wanted to hit the little keys and make lots of noise and hope something stuck or resembled some kind of a song. Eventually he crossed his arms and boycotted the lessons. For thirty minutes she'd go through the drills, explaining, demonstrating, but he wouldn't move. Finally she gave up on him. They haven't spoken since. The piano's still there in the living room. Sometimes when no one is in the house I'll pull open the lid that covers the keys and play *Jaws* as loud as I possibly can, over and over again.

So really when you gather it all up in a sack and take a look, it doesn't seem so bad. A wife, a kid, a town all to myself and a legacy I hold in my hands. A legacy shrouded in secret, protected by riddles and vague clues.

Chapter Nine

"BLAKEY, WE'RE HERE."

He opens his eyes. "No we're not," he says, looking around. "We're still driving." And technically he's right. We've just passed Harrisonville, Missouri which is a few miles outside Kansas City, but close enough. We've transitioned from flat Missouri farmland to the fields of concrete; gas stations, apartment complexes and car dealerships are now sprouting alongside the furrow of Highway 71.

Blakey has been to Kansas City once or twice that I know of. The last time was a few years ago. It was a special visit commissioned by Uncle Lou. Kansas City is our ancestral home. We've been there since Civil War days. Before that no one is sure about our roots. Irish, German are good guesses. Some have accused us of being part of an international Jewish conspiracy. It doesn't matter.

We started in the railroad business. The Shiloh's stole railroad tracks, then sold them back to the railroad companies when their trains ran out of track. Kansas City was the second busiest rail port in the country at the time, second to Chicago. Hell, we had Tom Pendergast working for us. He begged us to hand over some jobs that he could give to the people to keep their Greatly Depressed stomachs from making too much of a fuss. Tom worked in our great grandfather's office for awhile, right there at 1908 Main in the yellow brick building. Tom would make a proposal to our great grandfather, saying, "Mr. Shiloh, is this okay with you?" And my great grandfather would say, "Tom, I like you." And that meant there was still some detail that needed to be polished a bit.

Blakey turns his cell phone back on and says he has eleven missed calls, three new messages. He slides it back into his front pocket. "I'll listen to them later."

I take I-435 going west and then follow it as it curves northward and exit on 87th Street. Uncle Lou's house is in Lenexa, Kansas, a suburb fifteen miles southwest of downtown Kansas City. His barbecue restaurant is in south Kansas City, somewhere around 79th Street. I'm not going to bother calling Uncle Lou. I want to surprise him and, hopefully, surprise Birdshit and her boyfriend.

We pass a K-Mart and a McDonald's and Blakey says he's hungry, rolls down the window and fires up a Nugget. I turn left on Quivira and then take a left on 83rd Street and steer in and around the neighborhoods, where the roads blend and wind and turn into another road and it gets hard to keep track of which street we're on. But I see a sign for the Forest Woods subdivision and know that I'm in the right place. Wannabe McMansions capture more and more air. Big cars in the driveways. A few boats on trailers. I turn on Westgate Road and find his yellow house, second one on the right. There are no cars in the driveway. It looks like no one is home. But that doesn't mean anything. I park on the street.

"All right, Mr. Private Investigator. Now we're here."

"Guess you should go ring the doorbell and see if anyone's home. I'll wait here." Blakey fishes another Nugget out of his pack. It's bent. He examines it, straightens it out a little, then lights it. He blows the exhaled smoke in my face. I start to fake a cough and then figure it's not worth the bother.

"Why don't we both go up there?"

"You go," he says.

No one answers the door. I ring the doorbell, knock and even do the walk around the house bit people do even when it's obvious no one is home. I get back in the car. "My detective work is done. I've concluded that no one is home. What is your conclusion?"

"We'll wait. We'll wait all night if we have to. Someone will come home."

"Should we move the car? Park it down the street, so that it isn't obvious we're waiting?"

"If you want, it doesn't matter," Blakey says.

"It doesn't matter? I thought that would make perfect P.I. sense."

"Why? Because that's what they do on television?"

"No. Because it makes sense."

"Well, it doesn't."

Five minutes pass. I'm beginning to grow impatient. A lady jogging with a leashed beagle gives us a look.

"I have an even better idea. Let's go to Uncle Lou's restaurant. It's still early enough in the evening; they're probably still there. Proactive work, not just sitting and waiting like they do in the movies. And while we're there, we can get something to eat. I'm starving."

"Let's go." Strange how easily he was persuaded.

He puts his cell phone to his ear and dials into his voice mail. He listens to his messages, making no expression. No sighs, no smiles, no frowns, just listening.

It takes me almost forty-five minutes but I finally find Lou's BBQ somewhere near 74th and Wornall. The place is packed. People are standing outside. It's unclear whether they're waiting for a table or just standing around because they don't know what to do. I thought people in Kansas City were more "together" than this. There's no parking anywhere. I end up parking in front of a Blockbuster two blocks down the road. Blockbuster is busy too. We look like a suspicious pair, Blakey chain-smoking Nuggets and sneering at everyone who looks his way, me… well, from a small town in Arkansas. Our physical expressions alone bear no similarity whatsoever. We emote that something's-not-right feeling to everyone who walks past us. I see in the rearview a woman mouth Arkansas to herself. Yeah, I got an Arkansas plate. So what?

"Blakey, why is everyone looking at us?"

"I don't know. You're an old man driving a 10 year-old car."

"You already told me that."

"Well. We're also parked by the door and just sitting here."

"Should we get out?"

"I'd think so, if we want to go get ourselves a barbecue beef on a bun."

"And see if Birdshit is here."

"That too. But I'd rather eat first. Maybe we should pull out and drive back down, see if a spot has opened up by now. I bet one has."

"Yeah but what if there isn't a spot and we have to drive back here and do this all over again?"

"I don't think anyone is paying that much attention to us, Odom."

"Just wait. They are paying attention. Everybody is."

"Who?"

"You don't see it, Blakey. That's your problem."

"I ain't seeing nothing. And you need to relax. Let's just get out and go."

I open the car door and get out first. Blakey follows my lead, nods his head at several passersby. He tosses his cigarette directly in the path of an approaching family of five. Clean-cut, All-American and probably twice-a-week churchgoers; I'd wager a critical digestive organ that they're Overland Park residents. They first flinch and then fearfully jump over the cigarette like it's an angry Biblical serpent—all five of them, the father, mother and three boys—just one, two, three, four, five, like it's been rehearsed. When the last of them has made the jump, they all swat away the imaginary smoke smell that they believe must somehow be molesting them. They pat their clothes and shake their sleeves like they have bumblebees under their shirts. Then come the fake coughs. Two at first, then four. It is quite a performance.

Blakey and I walk across the parking lot, passing a shoe store, a quickie haircut place and a Mexican restaurant. We traverse some more concrete and then find ourselves stopped, hovering near the front door congestion. "Excuse me," Blakey says, gently pushing women and children out of the way. "How y'all doin? Doin alright?" I say, trying to make it clear we're not local. Aside from the "y'all," they must have been convinced; the group splits apart allowing Blakey and me through without incident

Once inside we pause and take it in, watching busboys scurry about wearing Lou's BBQ shirts and red ball caps. There are people sitting at every table in the place. It smells good. "Hi!" a teenaged girl screams and waves, clearly thrilled to be alive. Her smile big and sunny. "Welcome to Lou's BBQ! Just the two of you?" Before I have time to think, she says, "Right this way," pointing to the left. It's like suggestive selling; before you have time to come up with an answer you're already sitting down, sipping on lemon water, unwrapping silverware. Like at Wal-Mart before the sliding door closes behind you—no turning back - some old shit's pushing a cart at your crotch, telling you, Welcome, Welcome, Beautiful day, isn't? Thank you for coming… and when you leave, they say, buy-buy. Buy-buy. Buy-buy. It never leaves. It's always stuck in your head. At least Lou has invested in some young blood.

"We're looking for somebody," I say.

"Well," she smiles, playfully. "What do they look like and I'll help you find them." I survey the restaurant, my head slowly rotating like an oscillating fan. The kitchen staff is visible through an opening in the wall. They're wearing the same hats; sweat has entirely coated the bills.

"We can find them, thanks." We walk past her, straight towards the back, to Uncle Lou's booth in the far right corner of the restaurant. I see Lou's white-haired comb-over from the back. "There's our man," I say, nudging Blakey. "Can we smoke in here?" he says.

Uncle Lou is sitting by himself, head bowed, the *Kansas City Star* spread out in front of him.

"Lou-Lou!" He turns around and for a second it's clear has no idea what he's looking at.

"It's me, Odom."

"It is, isn't it," he says, standing up slowly from his booth. "And I see you brought along a surprise. Blakey Flake, the best P.I. in all of north-central Louisiana. Well, what in the devil has brought you boys all the way up here for?"

"Come on, Lou," I say, trying to break his act with a smile.

"What?" he says. "You boys hungry?" Blakey raises his hand and says that he is and asks if he can smoke in here. Lou says he can and Blakey does just that while reading the menu Lou handed him. Blakey's got the thing held about three inches from his face.

"Any closer and they call that Braille, Blakey," Lou quips, his humongous gut bouncing in unison with his loud, snarling laugh. Uncle Lou is a Kansas City native but he spent so much time in Arkansas, Louisiana and Mississippi during the old days of the Shiloh businesses that he stole a slight drawl for himself—a giddy Southern slur he sometimes regresses to in the presence of bona fide Southerners.

"I'll take beef on a bun, coleslaw, extra pickles and a Budweiser bottle. Make it two Buds." I tell Lou I'd have the same, minus the Buds. Iced tea is fine, unsweetened. Lou hollers down a passing waitress, repeats the order to her. She scribbles, head bobbing like a Japanese subordinate in a ninja movie.

The beers and iced tea arrive first. We've now established ourselves at Lou's special booth. Only Lou sits in it and you have to be invited to sit with him. Back in the day this is where the "job interviews" took place. Sometimes if the "interviews" weren't going too well or if the candidate was especially compelling, and some additional privacy was needed, they'd go downstairs and tell him to sit down in a guest chair bolted to the ground. This was where a "second interview" took place. The next room was where the rope, thick electrical tape, pointy objects and butane torch were kept. That was for a "third interview." As far as I know, everyone invited for a third interview is now permanently employed in the Shiloh Foundation.

"Seriously," Lou says, losing his laugh, almost turning serious, "what brings you two up here? Not that I'm not happy to see you boys."

Blakey passes the question to me. I always seem to be the spokesman, even though I'm busy squeezing a lemon through its fifth death, trying to get every drop of juice out of it. Blakey exhales a cloud of Nugget smoke, kills his first Bud in three gulps, throws the dead Nugget into the bottle, slides it away from himself and wraps his hand around his second one.

"Let's eat, Lou. We'll talk later," I say, taking a sip of my tea, testing it. "Why don't you fill us in on what you've been up to?"

"Well," Lou says, thinking, "I'm opening a new Lou's BBQ out in south Overland Park where all the assholes live. No one likes assholes but assholes sure like to spend money. So assholes who spend money eating my barbecue are okay with me." He laughs. Blakey smiles and takes a drink. I put a straw in my tea and drink it that way.

"But seriously," he says, "there's got to be a reason you two drove all the way up here. Blakey, why'd you come up all this way down from north-central Louisiana? You boys just driving around, taking a vacation? Oh and Odom I heard from your momma that you and your boys went 0-9 this last football season."

I pause for a moment. Lou called Momma. Well. He's family.

"Okay. Yeah. We're improving every year."

"Ever thought about pushing for an expansion of your role? Maybe jump up to assistant coach instead of the assistant to the assistant coach?"

"I haven't given it much thought."

"That may be the problem. The wrong people running things. You know what I mean?"

"I think so," I say, meeting his eyes.

"Leadership. Decision-making. Critical to an organization. That goes for any kind of organization."

"Sure," I say, nodding.

Blakey leans forward, "Just ain't like '86 is it, Odom? The famous 1-8 season."

"We tried scheduling the school for the blind the next year. Wanted to play them for homecoming. Apparently their bus got lost."

"So what's the occasion? I can't just sit here and not know what's going on." Lou says.

"We'll talk later, Lou. This is something that should probably be discussed," I lower my voice and lean in a bit, "down in the basement. You know?"

"Odom. What are you putting me up to? We're not going to the basement to talk. We can talk right here."

"No, Lou. This can wait. Not here."

The happy waitress puts our plates in front of us. Lou watches us arrange our forks in our hands and add sauce to our beef. When she walks off, Lou says, "We're not going to go talk in some musty, moldy basement. You boys can talk to me here, like normal people do. Lower your voice if you have to, but no one is paying any attention to us."

"Musty, moldy basement. You're funny, Lou."

"Enough of this, Odom. Let's talk about something else, like Gavin's film. Have you heard about that? We're all very proud of him."

"No," I say, "I don't think I recall anyone mentioning that."

"You'll be hearing about it if you haven't already," he says.

We eat. Nothing else is said. Lou skims the newspaper; Blakey orders another beer, smokes some more. I sit thinking about a death metal band I read about in the paper. Eventually it gets dark outside.

Chapter Ten

WHEN IT GOT NEAR closing time, Blakey, who was calling his eleventh Budweiser his third or fourth one, spilled the beans, letting Lou know why we had driven all the way up to Kansas City. Blakey took turns with his Nugget in his right hand and his Budweiser in his left, re-telling Lou the events of the past twenty-four hours. "So you see," Blakey said, "what it boils down to is that we're here because of a pretty girl. Imagine that." Lou straightened up, and said he had not seen or heard from Birdshit. Are you sure? I asked him. Have you checked your phone recently? She may have called sometime today. Lou examined his cell phone call log, shook his head. He asked around to see if anyone had called looking for him. Everyone shook their heads too.

At that point we'd been in the restaurant for over two hours. Lou really didn't say much. He listened, like he always did. Lou's a listener. That's why he's so wise. Eventually, I told him it was good seeing him and that I was glad things were going smoothly and wished him luck with the assholes in south Overland Park. I asked where I could find my half-deaf half-brother. Gavin's around, Lou said. He worked earlier in the day and would be back in the morning. We should drop by. He gave us his cell phone number. I asked how old Gavin was and Lou said thirty -one or thirty-two. No one knew for sure. Daddy wasn't clear on those sorts of things. I told Lou that I know there are other things he wanted to talk to me about, being at least a year since we'd been in touch. Maybe longer, Lou said, more like two years—but that really there wasn't much to say that hadn't already been covered. I know, I said, winking at him in a way he didn't catch, that we'd sit down and have a Shiloh talk. He said that's what we're doing, talking Shiloh talk.

"Lou," I said, "you're so damn good, you know that?"

Lou didn't seem to know how to respond to that.

Then I said, "Where the hell is Blakey?"

Lou flagged down the happy waitress and she smiles and says, "Nothing to worry about guys. He's just outside smoking and chit-chatting."

Lou says, "Thank you, Trisha."

When she walks off, Lou says, "Sorry I couldn't be of more help, Odom."

Uncle Lou's always here to help. He's my daddy's oldest brother. He was always the caretaker of the family. My daddy's the middle kid and the youngest is Uncle Vilonia who is no longer around either, like I've said already. I can tell Lou wants to say something about my daddy, share with me a memory or some endearing quality that he sees in me that reminds him of my daddy but he doesn't. He just takes another sip of his own unsweetened iced tea. It's funny, Uncle Lou never talks about Uncle V. And rarely mentions my daddy. It's his way, I suppose. No sense dragging in the past when the present is enough of a hassle.

I go outside and find Blakey standing there like Trisha said, smoking and chit-chatting with one of the young kids that works at the restaurant. I recognize the kid from earlier; he was bussing tables and cleaning the bathrooms. He looks to be eighteen or so. Blakey is lecturing him on the dangers of smoking cigarettes. The kid is smoking a cigarette himself, but he's not really smoking it. He's just sucking a hit of smoke into his mouth and then blowing it out of his puffed cheeks through the little circular hole he's formed with his lips. Meanwhile, Blakey kills an entire cigarette in four drags.

"And especially stay away from menthols. They got these menthol chemicals that crystallize in the lungs; they cause cancer and emphysema and all those diseases. It's not pretty. I've seen people with lung cancer and I can't think of a worse way to die."

The kid speaks. "I thought all that menthol stuff was bullshit."

"No, son, it's true. At least that's what they say."

"Yeah, but, sometimes I think *they* don't have a clue what's going on. And who are *they* anyway? We all say that. That's what *they* say; I hear *they* say, *they* say that. But who are *they*? No one knows. It's a convenient group to depend on but no one knows who *they* are."

"You've got a funny view on things, son, but I do say I like your version."

I pipe up. "Got yourself a new friend, Blakey?"

Blakey and this kid turn around, just now noticing. Blakey points to the kid's shirt. It's a red one that says LOU'S BBQ on it. "This kid says his work shirt is red because he gets dirty bussing tables and doing dishes. Barbecue sauce is red. Get it? I think that's pretty clever. If they wore green shirts or white shirts, he'd look like a developmentally challenged person."

"Very good," I tell Blakey, and go on to point out that the aprons and hats are red too. I haven't seen Blakey this inebriated in awhile. He's not quite drunk yet, just high and fuzzy. His eyes are smiling, his movements slow and calm. But it's downhill from here. Soon his eyes will turn half-shut, the movements unaccountable and the fuzzy becoming incoherent. He got drunk once at the bar in Frothmouth. I had to drag him out of there before something bad happened. Too many scrappers in that place.

"Have you finished your lecture on the dangers of smoking?" I ask.

"Yeah, I think." The kid throws his cigarette out into the parking lot and it rolls away. There are no other cars in the parking lot. The kid asks where we parked our car. It's in front of Blockbuster I say, pointing down the street.

"What's it doing down there?"

"We were going to rent a movie and decided barbecue sounded better."

"What were you going to rent?"

I look at Blakey. He shakes his head. I'm on my own again. Spokesperson.

"I don't know. We were going to look around. Why? Any suggestions?"

"Shit. I'm a big-time movie fan. I love movies. Someday I want to direct movies. Maybe write them. Or if all else fails, I'll act."

"My half-deaf half-brother is a documentary filmmaker. Blakey here is a movie buff."

"Used to be," Blakey says, correcting me. He shakes out a fresh Nugget from his pack and drinks from the beer he brought outside with him.

"What's your name?"

"Luke."

"As in *Cool Hand Luke?*" Blakey says.

"As in Luke Greenbrier."

"What do you do? You go to school? Work here full time?"

"I work here part time, actually. I'm a freshman at U.M.K.C."

Blakey coughs. "U.M.K.C., what does that mean?"

I explain, "It's the University of Missouri at Kansas City."

"What's he studying?" Blakey says.

"I don't know. Why don't you ask him."

"Hey kid. What are you majoring in?"

"Art History with a minor in Film."

"That's what Blakey studied in college."

"That guy went to college?" Luke says.

"He did," I say, confirming this indisputable fact. "Taught Survey of Art in the Western World at Middle Louisiana Community College, has an undergrad degree from Louisiana State University and a master's from Tulane. What am I leaving out, Blakey?"

"I was the recipient of the prestigious Babineaux Fellowship, awarded a Guidry Award two years in a row, a bunch of other grants and shit. Been so long ago I'd forgotten."

"What's your favorite kind of art?" Luke says.

Blakey ponders this for a moment. "I really like German Romanticism."

"That sounds like some made up shit," I say.

Luke says, "No, I've heard of it. What's your favorite painting?"

Blakey ponders again, then closes his eyes. "Probably, *The Monk by the Sea*, by Caspar David Friedrich. I consider it perhaps the boldest example of German

Romanticism as a whole. The theme of it, with the tiny figure of a man set against a natural landscape divided into three horizontal zones of color. At the bottom of the picture, the white sand dunes of the shoreline rise at an angle to the left. The tiny figure of a man robed in black is visible from behind—the only vertical in the picture. There is nothing else. The dark sea meets an extremely low horizon. Most of the painting is of the cloudy sky. Because all the lines lead out of the picture, infinity becomes the true subject of the painting. In the awareness of his smallness, the man, in whose place the viewer is meant to imagine himself, reflects upon the power of the universe."

He opens his eyes and notices the long ash hanging on his cigarette and knocks it off.

Luke looks at me. "This guy knows his shit."

"That sounds beautiful," I tell him, imagining it.

Blakey walks over to the newspaper stand. There are clearly no papers left. Thankfully he realizes this and does not push coins into the slot; rather he simultaneously tries to pull open the door while smacking the coin slot with his palm.

"Heeee yah!" he shouts. He tries again, trying to time his palm hitting with his yanking on the door. He's explained this to me before; if you do it just right, you can trigger the release mechanism and it opens. "Il-Yong Cha taught me this when I was a freshman at Louisiana State. He was from South Korea, a black belt in Tae Kwon Do. He could do this every time. He says it was about focusing your mind. You know that Seurat painting I mentioned at my trial, how solids could be full of holes? Well, that was him."

"Still practicing the technique, huh? All these years later," Luke says.

"Heeee yah!" Blakey shouts again. Nothing happens. "Screw it," he says, kicking the steel box with the toe of his cowboy boot.

I tell Blakey that we've got to get a move on; we need to go get a hotel room for the night. Our investigation will have to wait until tomorrow. Blakey's in bed with Budweiser and I'm so tired and besides that I have to make a major appearance at the restroom. Blakey pleads for a two-minute delay on our departure. He has to take one last piss before we get on the road.

"I'll tell you something you probably didn't know about Van Gogh," Blakey says.

"What's that?" Luke says.

"He's famous for what color?"

"Yellow."

"Right. You know how he got his yellow so soulful, so brilliant?"

"How?"

"He pissed it in."

"He did not."

"Look it up, kid. I'm telling you something you didn't know. The Greeks and Italians did the same. Especially the Italians. They'd use the urine of diseased people, which has a fuller yellow color. Look it up."

"I'll do that."

"And remember Michelangelo was quoted as saying that a beautiful thing never gives so much pain as does failing to hear and see it."

"Well, I better get in there and start stacking the chairs so we can vacuum and get out of here."

"Have a good one, Luke."

Luke goes inside and Blakey follows him in to use the bathroom one last time.

After a few minutes Blakey comes back out. He looks confused. I ask him what's wrong and he says nothing. This expression doesn't go away; he still looks unsure or worried. I ask him again. He says everything is fine. But I don't believe him. Something is wrong but I know I won't get it out of him until later or tomorrow.

"Where the fuck did we park," he says, walking aimlessly into the center of the lot.

"Blockbuster."

"Why the hell we do that?"

"I don't know, Blakey."

Chapter Eleven

THE DRIVE BACK to Lenexa will never end. Blakey's mouth is running on high gear. I see a Holiday Inn sign jutting up from the freeway. Two exits away. It's the same one I stayed at when we took trips in my youth. It was one of the original "Holi-Dome" hotels with the year-round indoor pool and saunas and hot tubs and croquet on an astro-turf patch in between the bar and lounge area. Thirty years ago when this place first opened, locals would book rooms to stay the night. They'd stay up all night splashing in the pool, playing putt-putt golf on the only hole and buying miniaturized shaving creams and tiny bars of soap out of the vending machine. Thirty years later, everything is still like this.

What's Blakey ranting about tonight? Oprah Winfrey.

"The number one culprit, the single most influential factor in our gradual social demise is due to this woman."

"What social demise?"

"I don't have time for all of that, Odom. But the point is that Oprah is the queen of mediocrity. That's what she sells and pushes: mediocrity, conformity, powerlessness, victimization. She tells people that we all have spirits. That we have individual spirits that have paths, preordained for our purpose. It's incredible horseshit, and people just gobble it up."

"She's a talk show host, Blakey."

"She's much more than a talk show host, my friend. She is the spokesperson for the invisible—Keep the People Down—movement that network executives and corporate bigwigs are all a part of. Keep us down, keep them silly, keep them following spirits and buying gadgets and self-help books. And you know what the most incredible part of it all is? The fact that people *believe* that they have guardian angels and a spirit that they must tap into or hang out with, get to know a little better. Like me and my spirit are going to go throw darts and reconnect. Gobble, gobble. You ever watch the local news? Probably not, but I do. All it is anymore is the goddamn weather. Right when the damn show begins, the weather guy comes on the screen with a "quick look" forecast and promises more good stuff later on. And then from then on out, every other reference is to the weather—the forecast coming up, in just a bit Ned will give you your forecast, we'll see how the weekend is shaping up. And not only that but the weather segment is half the program. Weather, weather, weather. That's it. We're a nation consumed by the weather, enamored with it, obsessed with it. What the hell for? No one is a farmer anymore. If the weather changes we can change our own environment with the flip of a switch. Look at Robert McCordery, your very own weather spotter. The guy is clinically insane now. His brain is now diseased and he can't speak of anything other than 'rain events,' 'possible thundersnows' and other meaningless weather descriptions. He's a prophet of our Godless age and in some ways he knows it. You ask him how's it going and he'll say: 'Be better if we didn't have a forty percent chance of rain developing this afternoon and an evening low of twenty two with the potential for snow and sleet developing in the overnight hours.' It's madness."

"Your point?" I say.

"The point is, weather is making us dumb."

How this relates to Oprah is anyone's guess. I turn on the radio, which I never do, and find a station playing songs that don't sound familiar. I leave it there. Blakey keeps talking but I can't hear him as clearly as before. The radio doesn't deter him from his verbal rampage. He skips around a lot when he talks. He's gone from Oprah to the weather; he goes from the weather to the meaning of happiness to why Steve Garvey has always royally pissed him off. I turn the radio down and say, "The baseball player?"

"Yeah, do you know of any other Steve Garveys that I could be referring to?"

"Well, fuck me running, Blakey. I was just asking."

"Steve Garvey is a twerp. He pisses me off. And don't bother asking why because I don't know why he does. He just does, always has. Maybe it's because he has big, fat, hairy forearms."

Next on Blakey's verbal hit-list are bad drivers, something about how cell phones have created an epidemic of bad driving. This epidemic breeds, he tells me. Then, finally, back to Oprah. "Oprah is a phony. The day she donates 50% of her income to charitable causes—what's that fifty million?—then I'll be impressed with her altruism and spiritually guided mission she talks about, holding a halo over her own head. Until then, she's nothing but a machine, a PR machine, nothing else. The woman donates pennies, damn pennies compared to her net worth." I turn the radio back up. He reaches over and turns it down, lights a Nugget. Smoke fills my car; I roll down my window.

"This smoke ain't going to kill you. It's going to kill me. Don't believe the secondhand smoke hype. It's all politics. I was just thinking, do you know what six words I dread hearing more than anything else? You want me to tell you?"

"Might as well."

"Don't you want to guess?"

"Nope."

"Okay. Ready? Those six words are: will you save some boxes for me."

"Huh?" I look over at him, like I heard it wrong.

"I can't stand it when people ask me to save boxes. Drives me nuts. You know why? Because I can *never* remember to do it. I can remember my ex-wife's birthday, oh yeah, but I sure as hell won't remember a week from now if you asked me to save you boxes."

"Why do people ask you this?"

"Dunno. All sorts of reasons."

"Those are your most dreaded words to hear? And that was seven words, not six." I turn the radio off and park the car in front of the Holiday Inn.

The reservation desk is empty when we enter. I ding the bell, wait, ding again. Finally a back door swings open and a grown woman in pigtails walks out, wiping her mouth. She asks if I have a reservation. I tell her I don't and she exhales loudly in this obnoxious way and goes to work typing on her keyboard. You'd think she was trying to write a Dear John letter the way she keeps typing, shaking her head, and typing some more.

"I only need one room, two beds. There's two of us."

"Sir, you'll be lucky if there's a room available. Now if you'll wait a moment, please."

"This your first day?"

"Excuse me? I've been employed here for two and half years."

"Do you go to a community college part time?"

"What is that supposed to mean?"

"Nothing. Just making conversation."

"This conversation is finished and as for your room request, we only have one available. A king."

"What does that mean, a king?"

"It means, sir, that it has one bed, a king-size bed. You want it or not?"

"Not really. But if that's all you have." She asks for my driver's license and reads it aloud to me, stopping at Frothmouth. "That's where you're from?"

"If that's what my State of Arkansas issued Class C driver's license says, then I'd probably err on the side that says that's probably right." I snatch it from her hands.

"You can just give that back because I haven't even entered it into the system yet."

I hand it back to her. She types, very slowly. Asks how I'm going to pay. Cash. She says no one pays cash anymore. I just quit answering her questions and stand there, holding some twenties in my hand, awaiting the total on the room. All I hear is ninety-something. I ask her to repeat it. It's a ninety-three-dollars-and-some-miscellaneous-change room.

"Ninety-three bucks? Does the bed vibrate and shoot bubbles out of the sides?"

She takes my cash and gives me six one-dollar bills and a nickel or two.

"Oh," she says, "did you prefer a non-smoking room?"

"That'd be nice."

"Unfortunately, Mr. Shiloh, this room is a smoking room. I'm so sorry."

She hands me my room key, a magnetized credit card, has me sign a piece of paper the size of a check and circles my room number.

"And your name is?" I say, reading SAMANTHA on her name badge.

"Samantha."

"Samantha, you've been a tremendous help. Thank you."

I get back in the car. Blakey is sound asleep. I drive the car around to the designated parking lot and pop the trunk. It is then that I realize we do not have any luggage. No toiletries, no overnight change of clothes, no toothbrushes, nothing. This is traveling at its finest.

Blakey wakes up when I slam the trunk closed. He wants to know where we are and then asks if there is any more beer. All gone, I tell him.

He wakes up enough to follow my lead inside and up to our room. I drop the room key into the slot and it opens on the first try, thankful for that little green light and clicking noise. I thought Samantha might have programmed the key incorrectly just to spite me.

Blakey is a master of the obvious; that's what makes him such a great private investigator, so he says. He contends that human beings complicate matters much more than they need to be. Most of what we need to know or what is important is obvious. So, of course, obviously there is only one bed in our room and Blakey wants an explanation pronto.

"First off, the good news is you can smoke in here."

"And the bad news is that we have to share the same bed."

"You got it."

"We don't have toothbrushes or clean underwear do we?"

I shake my head.

"Damn."

All of this just now dawns on Blakey. He lays on the bed, proclaiming his side, the one closest to the telephone and biggest of the room's four ashtrays. There are thirty channels on this television, Blakey says, reading the back of the remote control. He rattles them off in numerical order. He finds a channel and watches. A middle-aged bald man is talking about simplifying your life, condensing, solidifying, and recovering and moving past… Blakey says, "You see here. They think life is so simple and easy to figure out that it can be solved in one book. Or one appearance on television. They think their way is the only way, the right way, the solution."

We both watch for a few minutes without further comment. But I have to admit that I've been somewhat lured into this bald guy's bit. It would be nice if everything were so simple. And I can see how it's easy to buy into it. Because we want to believe, at least, I know I do.

"I'm going to sleep," Blakey says, nubbing out his goodnight cigarette in the ashtray. He turns off the light; the glow from the television is the only light in the room.

"See you in the morning, Odom."

"Goodnight." On the television screen is a movie I've seen before but can't remember the name of. I try to remember but then give up, turn it off and lay down next to Blakey.

"Don't worry," Blakey's voice says, coming at me from all directions in the darkness, "Everything will be all right. I promise. There are a lot of people who care a lot about you."

The next thing I know the telephone is ringing. Blakey doesn't hear it and I have to reach over him to answer it. As I put the phone to my ear I see the clock on the table. It's 4:30 in the morning. I say hello and there is a pause but I can tell someone is there. "HELLO THIS IS YOUR WAKE-UP CALL. HELLO. THIS

IS YOUR WAKE-UP CALL. HELLO. THIS IS YOUR WAKE-UP CALL."

I hit zero for the front desk. A man answers. "Hey! I just got a wake-up call. I didn't request a wake-up call." There is some kind of giggling commotion going on, it is muffled but I can hear laughter, then I hear what sounds like someone saying, "It's him."

"Hello. How can I help you?"

"Samantha?"

"This is she. What seems to be the problem?"

I unplug the phone, get up and make sure the door is locked from the inside and go back to sleep.

The best sleep is when you wake up without any kind of worldly connection, when you don't remember going to bed or anything else in between, finding the pristine darkness that doesn't necessarily exist anywhere. That's how you know you're one tired sack. I don't dream much. The few dreams I do have tend to be recurring and I wouldn't bother sharing those picture-shows with anyone. Show me someone who talks about their dreams and I'll show you someone who has given up. The same goes for numerology enthusiasts, UFO convention attendees and members of "living fulfilling lives" cults. And anyone who says they can move objects by staring at them. Turn around and walk the other way from these folks. Don't even give them the satisfaction of saying, "Really?"

Mona, my ex-wife, became a believer in past lives and went to this regression therapist in North Little Rock once a month. This fascination arose when I told her that I didn't think our present lives were doing much good for either one of us. I put the idea of a divorce on the table, laid it there quietly and left the room. It stayed on that kitchen table for over a year before anything was done about it. Anyhow, if you got Mona talking on this subject she'd tell you she used to be the sister of so-and-so who was a famous leader or dictator. And before that she was married to a powerful military man of some notoriety. She even dragged me along one time; I went because I didn't mind the drive.

The office was very comfortable. And I say that largely because of the abundance of pillows. They were everywhere. And the wattage of the light bulbs couldn't have topped 10 or 15 watts. It was near dark in every room. It was odd and it kept you off balance because your brain craved light and clarity but the setting was dim and secretive.

Under hypnosis—actually I fell asleep and snored for an hour—the therapist said that I reported to her that I was a seamstress in Norway. This is bizarre because if you asked me to name the first twenty countries that came to mind, I don't think Norway would make that list.

There was this support group after my session in which myself and Mona and six other whack jobs sat on bean-bags and comfy chairs and discussed our past lives findings. The real cultist in the group, a forty-something named Carl, had elaborate past life histories that he explained in great detail. And me, the only skeptic in the bunch, had to stand up and report that I used to sew sweaters in the snowy hills of Norway.

When I finally pull my eyes open for good—after a series of attempted wake-ups—Blakey is laying on his back next to me with both hands tucked behind his head; his "deep thought" posture. "Morning, Blakey," I say, yawning, and folding my hands behind my head.

"I've been up for three hours already," he says.

"What time is it?"

"Almost 9:30."

"What's going on? Have you heard from anybody?"

"I've got two messages on my phone but I haven't listened to them yet."

"Tell me, Blakey, do you ever take your phone off silent so that you can actually hear when someone is calling you?"

"Why would I?"

"Right," I say. "Of course, what a stupid thing to do."

Then he says, "Do you ever miss being a kid? The adventure, the risk-taking, the unpredictability of youth. The not knowing what is going to happen next. The way we used to live."

"I don't think I think about it like that. It just is what it is. I mean, one day you're a kid and then one day you're not a kid anymore. I'm not sure when that happens, but it does."

"I sure do miss it. I miss it, I think, because I know my years are numbered now. When you're younger you never die. Maybe that's why I've done all these different things. I know that this is it. My one chance. My one life. There's nothing after this. I think it's probably good that there aren't more people like me in the world."

"What do you mean?"

"Believing in a life after this one keeps most people in their place. Keeps them showing up to their jobs, the toilets flushed, the roads repaired, food at the grocery stores."

I get up and use the bathroom. I sit on the end of the bed and flip on the TV.

Blakey says, "You know why I'm an atheist? The short version is I'd taken a bunch of drugs, this was when I was a teenager, and had been drinking heavily. Most people find God under these kinds of influences but I found that there was no god. Funny, isn't it? But really I've been an atheist since I was six years old."

"You were six?"

"Yep, six years old. It was so simple and obvious. But, most people, as you know, fail to recognize the obvious."

"My daddy always said that a guy named Rich killed God. He said Rich wanted everyone else to believe there was a god even though there was no such thing, so he could dupe people and make money off of them. He said Rich lived in a gated underground community with other people like him. And that all the people above ground, you and me and everybody else, all of our work went to providing goods and services to Rich. Daddy said that we weren't really free. That we just thought we were but it was all a joke. Anyhow, I used to believe all this stuff. I don't know what I believe anymore."

"Believe the obvious."

"Do you think there are ultimate truths in this world, Blakey?"

"I'm not a cultural relativist but I do think that truth, at least in the way human beings understand it, has had different versions at different times."

"What do you mean?"

"Like a story or movie that goes through editing. What is true right now may end up being completely false in a hundred years. Just think about what we thought was true a few hundred years ago, how the mind worked and space and physics. All of those truths were turned on their head."

"But eventually you get to a point where you figure it out, right?"

"Theoretically, yes. And I think that's what you mean by ultimate truths or mathematical platonic truth, where there's an ultimate reality or truth out there that has to be deciphered first. But I don't think we'll make it that far. We have way too much fun killing each other and inventing silly beliefs and fucking everything up more than we truly care about truths. You know, that person who gets things going for themselves for a little while but then goes and just fucks it all up. That's what humanity is. That person."

"What do you think about what my daddy believes?"

"I don't know. Your daddy was a little off-kilter to put it mildly. But on the other hand, I was listening to you when we were driving up to Kansas City. Nowadays there are people who live underground, like those people running the computers. People with a lot of power. When your daddy was first saying these things thirty years ago there was no such thing. Except for missile silos."

"Tell me, what's it like to be you, Blakey?" I shake my head, close my eyes and open them.

"A long time ago, instead of making a list of things I wanted, I made a list of things I could live without and the longer that list became the happier and freer I felt. That was the way I wanted to feel all the time."

"The simple life."

"Well," he laughs. "It hasn't always been simple. But the point is that my default position so to speak is easier to find and less stressful to maintain. No matter what, I've been able to strip myself of so much and still find contentment."

"You mean happiness."

"Odom, the people on a quest for happiness never find it."

"Change of subject before I forget. What was bothering you last night?"

"Last night? Nothing."

"No, I mean right when we left Lou's. You went back in to take a piss and when you came out it was like you'd seen a ghost or something."

"Ohhh. Yeah."

"Oh, yeah, what?"

"Oh, nothing. I forgot. I don't remember much from last night."

"Shut the hell up. You weren't that drunk. You remember."

"Okay. I just haven't had time to figure it out or think about it yet. That's why I haven't said anything. I just woke up. I'll tell you later."

"You woke up three hours ago."

"What I'm thinking is Lou isn't playing straight with us. He knows more about Birdshit than he's leading us to believe."

"What makes you think that?"

"Last night, when I went back inside to take a piss, I heard him on the phone."

"What? Talking about Birdshit?"

"No, talking *to* Birdshit."

Chapter Twelve

AFTER SHOWERING AND checking out, we drive to Lou's. The sunny, smiling waitress tells us he hasn't arrived yet. Blakey gets a table and orders onion rings and a side of dill pickles. It's the early end of the lunch rush and there are only three tables occupied. A man and his girlfriend fight in a corner booth over who is the bigger asshole. Apparently they're both terrible at relationships, however some justice must be served and that favorable judgment will go to whoever comes across as less of an asshole than the other.

I tell Blakey, "I think I see Gavin. Over there."

"It is him," Blakey says, peeling the batter-fry off an onion ring. Blakey yells his name across the restaurant. Everyone but Gavin looks at us. He yells again, louder this time.

"He's half-deaf Blakey."

"But I'm really yelling. He should be able to hear me." Blakey cups his hands around his mouth and shouts. "Gavin!" "Gavin! Hey! Gavin!"

A waitress taps Gavin on the shoulder and points at us. He looks over and his eyes get real big and excited and he marches right over. I stand up to greet him. Blakey stays seated; Gavin wraps an arm around my shoulder and squeezes. I pat him back, an awkwardly half-brotherly kind of thing. We rarely see each other and when we do it's exciting for about eight seconds before everything goes back to normal.

"What on earth are you both doing up here?"

Blakey lights a Nugget. "We're working."

I ask Gavin about his documentary. I tell him Lou was making a stink about it, and how proud he is. Then I repeat everything, word for word.

"Really? Proud, huh? Well, you guys have great timing because my premiere is tonight. You want to come?"

"Yeah, maybe Lou did say that. Sure."

Blakey says, looking at me, "What's it about again?"

"Well," he says, "I have this obsession with failure. I want to expose failures, people who had big dreams or had their shot and they never fulfill it, sometimes by their own doing, sometimes by bad luck or whatever. It fascinates me because really most of us are failures; we never come close to what we want to be. And we're too afraid to admit it."

"I don't think I agree with that," Blakey says.

"I know you don't. No one agrees with me. But it's true."

"What my half-deaf half-brother is trying to say is that he is banking on being a success by documenting failures. Interesting way to swing at a pitch, ain't it?"

"Sounds silly to me," Blakey says, going back to his onion rings and pickles.

Gavin goes on to explain that he works at Lou's five days a week, prepping in the morning and cooking through the lunch rush and then spends the rest of his time editing the film back at his apartment. He's gone through most of his Shiloh money financing previous films. He's counting on this one actually making him some money. He's tried his hand at low-budget horror films. One of which was a twenty-nine minute bloodfest about a killer roller skate that rides around town after dark, smashing peoples' skulls with its metal toe guard. His film, *Two Weeks Ago Tomorrow*, a psychological head-scratcher that made no sense, even after ten viewings, was shown at two regional film festivals, one at the "Land of Oz" film festival in Emporia, Kansas and the other in Springfield, Missouri at the Southwest Missouri Film Competition. The idea behind the film was that when the main character, Ivan, woke up everyday it was really two weeks ago tomorrow, hence the title. The current day was never clear but Ivan always knew that tomorrow would be two weeks ago or something like that. Apparently, per Gavin's "spoiler" Ivan is either stuck in some kind of mental mind trap or else is haunted by an invisible poltergeist. Or else it was a cinematic parody of some kind of bad self-help book. It was terrible. His documentaries have been better. He did a short-short (which is basically a five minute film) about the history of the

IntelliVision game system; in *Nadia Rock* Gavin traced the beginnings of the Romanian punk rock movement which began in February of 1983 and was pretty much over by August of the same year. He had some success with this and followed up with a documentary on the forever-ago-forgotten band, Warlock, whose one hit, "All We Are" was an MTV staple on the Headbangers Ball. This little film actually won him a $5,000 grant from a filmmaking foundation in Los Angeles; thus, here we are today. I try to interpret these strange movies as a manifestation of his deafness, or near deafness but my powers of interpretation aren't up to task. Maybe I should ask Blakey.

"Is this the final version of the film we're gonna see?" I ask.

"Almost. I have a few more tweaks left but I hope in the next few weeks, maybe a month at most, I will be completely finished."

"What else is going on?"

"That's about it. I'd better get back to work. I see more people coming in. We'll be slammed in about thirty minutes. We'll chat later on. Good seeing you, big half -brother."

"Have you seen Lou?" Blakey asks.

"Not yet," Gavin says and walks to the kitchen.

The tables fill up with business casual diners. Trisha flies from table to table taking orders. Two other waitresses I don't recognize work their tables too. Through the front door comes Luke Greenbrier. He's carrying his apron, rolled up in a ball. He walks back into the kitchen. Blakey smokes and reads the *Kansas City Star*. I tell Blakey that his friend Luke has arrived. Blakey looks up, doesn't see him and goes back to his paper. Luke emerges from the kitchen, tying his apron behind his back. He picks up a bus tub and white rag and stands at the bussing station and watches the waitresses move about. He stands there, waiting for something to do.

I wave him over. He strolls across the restaurant floor and sits in the booth next to us. Blakey says hi and continues to glance through the newspaper.

"How was school today?"

"All right, I guess."

"What time does Lou usually show up?"

"It depends. He doesn't have any set time. You see him when you see him, as he likes to say."

Blakey looks up, holding his paper still in his hands. "Say Luke, what do they pay you here? Six bucks an hour or so?

"About that, plus the waitresses tip us out some."

"Do you like it?"

"It's okay. I'd rather be doing something else. But that goes for most folks who work in kitchens."

"You get along with Lou pretty well? Does he trust you?"

"Yeah, he's a good guy. I think he knows me pretty well. It's been a year and a half since my job interview."

"Have you ever thought about doing investigative work?"

"What kind of work do you mean?"

"Investigations. You know, asking questions, following people around, that sort of thing."

"That sounds like something I'd be interested in."

I see where Blakey is going and let him go with it. He thinks Luke can give us an inside track on Lou and what may be really going on. I'm starting to get a little skeptical about Blakey's methods, but all right. Maybe we'll at least find out what happened to the basement.

"Blakey and I won't let this get in the way of your schoolwork."

"Fuck school. I need a break anyhow."

"No, no, no," Blakey says. "This isn't a break from school. This is a temporary job, a part time thing."

"Working for who, you guys?" Luke says.

"That's right."

"So I'm hired?"

"You're hired," Blakey says, folding up his newspaper. "Oh and this is just between the three of us. No one else knows that you're working for us or with us."

"How much are you going to pay me?"

Blakey puts the newspaper down, taps his lighter on the table, "Will you listen to this kid? How does ten bucks an hour sound?"

"That'll work. What do you want me to do?"

"Nothing yet. But you work for us now. Keep your eyes and ears open at all times. Stay awake. We'll have something for you to do soon."

As much as I don't want to, I step outside and call Bree because I know I'm bound to do it by some threadbare sense of husbandry. I've got this little phone with big fat numbers that works well enough. But there are reasons I don't call as often as I should. I don't have a fancy unlimited calling plan or anything like you see joyfully advertised on television. Where we live it's hard to get dependable service and usually those companies and plans are a waste of money—all the dropped calls and the minute after minute, dollar after dollar spent yelling into the phone, "Hello? You there? Hey? Can you hear me? Hey… is that you? You still there?" I only buy small increments of minutes, usually thirty or forty at a time. I like to save them for an emergency. It's also convenient when I need to disconnect.

I get her on the phone. The sound of her voice gives me a sinking feeling. I ask her to check on Momma for me. I tell her I know Momma's got to be a wreck by now. Bree asks why it took so long for me to call and asks where I am. I ignore her questions. I asked her how Sparky's doing.

"He's fine. I'm fine too. Thanks for asking."

"And Momma?"

"Your Momma's fine too. Which is a surprise. I figured she'd be up living in the trees by now. She's actually been getting by all right. Other than when she's mouthing off about how worried she is about you and that sister of yours."

"Bree. Momma doesn't mouth off. What's she doing?"

"Just watching her shows and taking it easy."

"Anything happen I should know about?" I say.

"Like what?"

"I don't know. I'm just checking in. Any mail or anything?"

"Just bills and stuff."

"Any magazines?"

"A few."

"Which ones?"

"Well, shit. I dunno. I just set them on the table next to your chair in the living room."

"Sparky doing all right in school?"

"Yeah. I told him all about the moon today. Say, when you coming back?"

"Pretty soon. We haven't had any luck finding Birdshit yet. But we're getting close."

"Where are you?"

"We're in Kansas City."

"I'll tell them boys that's where you are then."

"What boys?"

"These nice gentlemen in suits and mustaches have come by twice looking for you. I told 'em I didn't know where you were at, which was the truth. Now I know."

"Who are they?"

"They are with the Arkansas State Police and someone from Tennessee too."

I feel chill-bumps on my back and arms.

"You there?"

"Yeah."

"So you mind telling me why the police are looking for you? Now don't get me wrong, they been real nice to me and I been real nice back. I can't figure you done anything too awfully bad. You didn't get online and try to get yourself some little fifteen year-old girl to roll around with you did you?"

"Oh, God, no."

"Then what is it?"

"It's nothing."

"Two visits from law enforcement folks in suits and unmarked cars from two states doesn't sound like nothing. Odom, are you gonna tell me or not?"

"Let me call you back a little later on."

She hangs up on me. It could have been worse.

Chapter Thirteen

BACK INSIDE, BLAKEY is sitting in Lou's booth. He seems to have officially taken over. I don't know how wise this is and scan the restaurant for Lou. The chain of command is very rigid and must be respected. I don't know what to think so I ask Blakey if I can sit down. He nods his head and asks if I called Bree. I tell him everything is fine.

He says, "While you were outside on the phone, Luke got wind of the fact that Lou isn't coming in at all today. Taking the day off, according to Luke. I've been told he never does that. I think we found our little fishy to follow."

"Who, Lou?"

"Damn right." Trisha puts a Budweiser in front of Blakey and makes sure he sees her smiling at him. Blakey winks at her. He takes a small drink, savors the taste, closes his eyes and says, "Ahhh." He reaches for his pack of Nuggets and I get up and go to the bathroom, lock the door behind me, put my hands on the sink and stare at myself in the mirror, like characters do in the movies when they're up shit creek. The cops are looking for me. I wonder what for. I mean, I know what for.

I unlock the bathroom and leave. Blakey is still sitting, a vaguely peaceful expression on his face. I ask him if he has a copy of today's *Kansas City Star*. "Right here," he says, handing me a mess of newsprint. It's all out of order and this annoys me for a moment while I turn pages right side up and get it situated into some semblance of its original nature. I find the sports section and scan the stories, on the lookout for news about a French cyclist who got run over by a car in downtown Memphis, Tennessee. I'd imagine I wouldn't miss it if such an article existed. I don't find one. I turn back through it again, backwards, like Arabic and Hebrew readers do.

I stick the sports back where it belongs, in between the Business and Metropolitan sections.

"What are you looking for?"

"Nothing," I say. Blakey eyes me through the smoky veil that separates us. The smoke drifts and lingers like a post-battle scene from the Civil War. "I'd say you were looking for something," he says.

"Oh, nothing. Just thought I might glance at what dogs were racing today."

"You want to go to the dog track."

"Maybe, if we find Birdshit."

"Well, open that back up. We got time. When do the afternoon races start?"

"I'll look at it in a bit."

"I mean it's hard to believe a yokel sport like dog racing made it all the way up here."

"Sure is."

"But that ain't what you were looking for, Odom. You and I both know it."

"Does Lou get ESPN on that television?"

Trisha walks by and overhears. "That up there," she points, "hasn't worked since I graduated from high school."

"When was that, sweetheart?" Blakey says.

"1991."

"You a young one in an old package, ain't you?"

"I'm hardly old, Mr. Blakey," she says, with a hand on her hip. Blakey passes on a follow up comment; it's too far north for one of his charming Southernisms. Instead he waves his cigarette in front of his mouth, landing it in between his lips after three or four thoughtful seconds.

"That's what I thought," and she walks off, bouncing it up high, left and right. She stops, pivots and comes back to us. "You two coming to Gavin's premiere tonight?"

"I forgot about that," I say. Luke joins us, sitting down quietly, unwrapping his apron from around his waist.

"It's at the old Glenwood Theater. There's a pre-party somewhere. I don't know where yet. I'll get the details."

Blakey shrugs, "I guess we'll go."

"I was hoping you were going," Trisha says, looking Blakey straight in the face. "Thought you might give me a ride," and walks off again, the same left and right bouncing.

"We're going," he says and then he says it again, "Oh, yeah, we're going."

I went back to the Holiday Inn and signed up for another night. There was a different person working the desk, a young guy. I asked if I could have the same room. He informed me that it had not been cleaned yet. I told him that was fine, to forego cleaning the room so that I could take an afternoon nap. All I need are clean towels and a little bar of soap. I go in. Blakey's cigarette butts, bent and dead, jut up from the glass tray like Medusa's hair.

Blakey was still sitting in the booth with Luke when I left. They assured me they were going to get some work done. Then they were going to go run around town, maybe see a movie or visit the Nelson-Atkins Museum of Art.

The only sleep I get is in little bunches of ten- or fifteen-minute increments. I close my eyes and wake up thinking it's been longer, only to discover I'd been asleep for exactly twelve minutes. I turn on the television in the room and leave it on ESPN. They're showing tennis from some European clay court. Women in short white skirts making little grunts. I'm waiting and watching for an ESPN Newsbreak to cut into someone's serve to tell me that Pierre Dupont of Paris has died from wounds suffered in an accident and that the police have upped their investigation, bringing in national law enforcement agencies. Then what do I do? I think. If that happens. It hasn't yet. But if it does. I feel my mind begin to roar and swirl like it does sometimes; like one of those carnival rides where you go around and around stuck to the wall and then the floor goes out from under you—just a pair of eyes observing some distorted version of reality that never adds up. But I clench my fists and deliberately distract my thoughts. I think about concrete things, about my Honda of the year 1997, about the road I just drove in on, what this hotel looks like, the salt and pepper shakers at Lou's restaurant; concrete images that are real and won't bleed and won't deform and turn into something else like a magician's trick. Eventually, I fall asleep.

Sometimes it so happens that events occur for a reason; even though this is false, it is an excellent thing to consider. For example, at the precise moment that I sit up in my bed and turn up the volume on the television, one of the ESPN commentators says that the full story on Pierre's condition will air on SportsCenter tonight at 10:30 central time. The hotel clock registers 4:45. When I glance back at the television, the channel has mysteriously shifted to Oprah. And I'm not surprised to find Oprah holding a book in front of the camera. Lately I've noticed that silence creates things that I wonder if I should be hearing. I turn the volume up and I get in the shower. Oprah's voice carries over the stream of water pouring from the spout.... "Andrew's amazing story is all recounted in splendid detail in his book *Other Voices*. I'm telling you now to go buy this book. It's so incredible and it will simply take your breath away. What he had to endure and the years of therapy needed to repair it. You could say, repair, couldn't you, Andrew? Is that a good word?

"Oprah that's the perfect word. In fact, I use it extensively throughout the book. In fact, Chapter One is titled, 'Repair the Damage Done To You.' "

"Would this book benefit someone who's had no damage inflicted on them?"

"Absolutely. There's an appendix in the back titled, 'Nothing's Wrong, Huh? Think Again.' And in it is a simple worksheet you can use to find the damage."

"Amazing. I urge everyone to go out and get this book. We're all damaged, aren't we?" The crowd roars back a thunderous barrage of screams and claps. "Exactly. We all need to be repaired. Coming up after the break, Andrew will talk about how he was able to discover his secret place—as he calls it—and describe what he found there."

The water coats me. I splash it on my face and reach for the soap and realize they didn't restock it. I pull back the shower curtain and listen some more.

When I get out I check my phone and immediately call Blakey back since he's called ten times.

"Where have you been?"

"I took a shower."

"Odom, swing by here and eat with us. Then we're off to this pre-party for Gavin's premiere."

"I'll be there in a bit. Have to finish my shower. Have you found out anything about Birdshit? Lou? Anything?"

"No, Luke and I did a little observation work today but nothing that has brought us much information. We went to the Nelson-Atkins and the Kemper Museum of Contemporary Art. Good stuff."

"I bet it is good stuff, Blakey."

"Well, quit yapping and get over here."

"I'll be there."

Chapter Fourteen

BLAKEY'S INVESTIGATION HAS LED him to a cocktail party. The pre-premiere festivities are taking place at a huge apartment inside the Western Auto building in downtown Kansas City. It takes up half of an entire floor. There are more people here than I expected. There's a band in the corner with this little girl playing this big standup bass. She's singing too. It sounds like old rockabilly stuff. I watch for a while as her right hand plucks the strings and her left marches up and down the fretboard. She gives me a wink and I look down and go find Blakey and Trisha. They've been standing close to each other every chance they've had since we first got to town.

He's smoking a cigarette, as usual, and discussing the finer points of the investigative work he does. I listen. When he's done he surprises everyone, including me, when he announces that he's retiring.

"What?" I say. Trisha looks at me and so do the other people standing around him.

"I've got bigger dreams than this. I've put in my two-week notice, you could say. Have to make a few phone calls, settle things down at HQ. Don't worry. We'll finish the deal we got cooking here but after that the Bald Eagle's gonna build his nest in the north."

"What are you gonna do?"

"Don't know yet. Thought about opening a restaurant of my own maybe. Or doing some traveling. Always wanted to be a stand-up comic too. Might give that a try."

"A comedian? You have bills to pay Blakey. Why don't you go back to teaching?"

"Might. I don't have many bills to pay, just what I need to live on, get by. You know that."

Trisha says, "I think you'd be a great comedian with all your experience and wisdom."

"You're right about that," he says, finishing his cigarette.

Luke appears from around a corner and joins us. Blakey puts an arm around his shoulder and they rehash their visit to the art museums earlier in the day. Trisha glows under Blakey's shadow and takes a deliberate step forward, closer to him, so that her left arm is only an inch or two from his. And every so often he gently collides into her and she absorbs the blow and her cheeks redden. I slip away from the group. I am surrounded by strangers. Every age group, sex, ethnicity and physical appearance is represented at this place. Everyone is talking but no one is listening. The smiles are performances and the physical attractiveness hierarchy is constantly being challenged by new arrivals. As I listen it seems no one is satisfied with anything. There is a lot of complaining and nitpicking. Not like in Froth-mouth where complaints are few. A lot of the talk is about restaurants, resorts and travel destinations, a lot of which sounds like rehearsed dialogue: The lack of adequate plumbing and the limitless insects. I wander back over to where the band is playing. I sit down, leaning against the brick wall.

I don't do parties very well. I'm a loner by nature. Bree always handled these affairs better than I do. I always leaned on her in social situations. I wish she were here so I could get up off the floor and feel comfortable actually engaging people in conversation. I kid her about not being too bright but she's smarter than I give her credit for. She didn't get too far in schooling but she's got the same set of feminine instincts that all women have. She knows something's going on before it happens. I don't know if I'll tell her about Pierre. I suppose if he dies, I'll have to tell her.

I keep watching the bassist. The little girl playing isn't really a little girl; she looks tiny for some reason. I imagine her pretty card used to have a high limit, I wonder how much she has left on it though. If I've learned anything from Gavin's previous documentaries, it's that a life in music can wreak havoc on how many more purchases you have. Those minimum payments keep getting higher and higher.

Her age is unclear, mid or late 20s. The older I get the harder it is for me to gauge a person's age. When I was younger I could confidently place people in the correct category: early 20s, mid 30s, late 40s, etc. I'll be 40 later this year.

Whatever that means.

Gavin arrives with his two dates, one on each arm, a blonde and a redhead, although they are not particularly attractive. When the redhead says something, Gavin turns to steady his eyes on her lips and says, "Say it again." She does and he says, "Talk more slowly, sweetie." She leans in and is practically tonguing his ear. He gently pushes her off and says, "I said talk more *slowly*, so I can see your lips. Not talk more *closely*."

A big fuss is made over his arrival. Cameras click and a news reporter and cameraman appear, his face illuminated by the bright light, a microphone in his face. I can't believe it. I didn't know my half-deaf half-brother was a local cinematic celebrity. He tells the reporter that he plans to submit the film to every conceivable festival and expects a distribution deal will result. This is where the bucks start rolling in, he says, laughing. Then he excuses himself and escorts his two third-tier beauties to the bar. He walks past me and says, "So glad you could make it big half-brother." The beauties look at me without expression and turn away. Blakey, Trisha and Luke follow too. They stand around the bar, waiting for their orders to be made, bottle caps popped off.

The music stops and the tiny bass player announces that they're taking a fifteen -minute break and the band heads to the bar. The bass player fidgets with the amps and effects pedals and the various chords. I start to say something but the sound doesn't come. I cough and try again. "That was good."

"Thank you," she says, smiling, looking down at me.

"Very nice. I enjoyed it." Then I remember I'm sitting on the floor.

Luke breaks away from the pack and sits down next to me. He hands me a foam plate with pretzels and chips and salsa on it. "I'm not hungry. Thanks, though." I set it on the floor next to me. "So Blakey is retiring, huh?"

"Yeah," Luke says. "He told me that today. We were standing at the top of the steps outside of the Nelson and he said that he was going to be making some changes in his life."

"That sounds like him. He makes drastic changes every few years. I wonder how he does it. All I know is that I don't change much. Actually, I've never changed anything."

Luke listens, nods his head through the silence.

"So," I say, "you two get along pretty well?"

"It's funny how well we get along."

"I'd say so."

The tiny bass player approaches. She's holding two beers. She steps closer and says, "You want to come have a drink with me?"

"Sure." I stand up. I take the beer she holds out for me. Luke says he'll talk to me later. "How'd you learn to play so well?"

"Practice."

"How many years have you played?"

"Fifteen."

"And you've always sang too?"

"Yes."

"Do you ever give answers that are more than one word long?"

"You're asking questions with one word answers." I follow her out of the main room, past the bar into an adjoining room where only a few people are scattered about, mostly smokers, who have isolated themselves for courtesy's sake. "Do you mind?" she says, taking out a pack of her own.

"Oh, no. Not at all." I take my first sip of the beer I've been holding. It tastes like beer, a taste I never fully acquired. I'm careful not to make a face when I drink it. She puts it down like a veteran. I look closely at her face and figure her to be thirty. From a distance her small stature shaves off years from her appearance, but up close her smile is slightly worn, her eyes dark from too many smoky rooms. Her fingers are polish-less, nails cut short.

She holds her beer up for a toast. I click bottles with her and drink. "A little company never hurt anyone." I agree.

"You look like you need some company," she says. I stand there with nothing else to say. Occasionally I try to get a better look at her when she's not noticing. A woman says hi from across the room. She waves. A guy comes up and whispers in her ear, she pats him on the back and says, "Oh, Derek, you never quit. Get out of here."

"He's my drummer," she says, drinking her beer. "I'll be right back." She drops her cigarette into an abandoned bottle. I wait around for ten minutes but she doesn't come back.

I rejoin the main room and see the tiny bass player and her band in their corner where they grab sticks, shoulder back into guitars. She starts pulling on the bass strings, singing *Love, love, my love, always leaving me*, into the microphone.

Uncle Lou is now standing with Blakey. The crowd has grown considerably since I was away. It's a tighter fit, more bodies I have to excuse myself around to make my way through the crowd. Uncle Lou is laughing and I see Blakey coming my way. He approaches, not slowing down, steps out of my way. I grab him. "Blakey what's going on?"

"I'm going to the bathroom," he says, "these beers are running right through me. Did I tell you that I've retired as of two minutes ago? Our work is done thanks to Luke and Uncle Lou. I'm afraid the hardest part has just started for you. But my part is done." He tries to walk past me but I grab him again.

"What are you talking about?"

He turns, holds out his arm, and points in the direction he came from. "Birdshit. She's standing right over there."

Something doesn't feel right. The first drips of paranoia return. I feel like I'm on the receiving end of a giant, well-played practical joke. Or like one of those characters in old sci-fi movies when they return to earth out of sync with humanity, clueless to everything going on around them.

There she is, standing twenty feet away, talking to a pair of men in suits, enjoying herself. I see Michael standing next to her. Birdshit should be in big trouble but everyone is acting like I'm the one who is out of the loop. I continue to stand still, staring at everything, absorbing the music that is playing behind me, feeling the music push me towards her. And for the first time I notice how many people are watching me. It seems like everyone is in on it. I hear my name being whispered in covert conversations.

If I wait long enough—then it happens. She sees me and immediately slips away from the suited men.

"Hi, Odom. How are you?" She gives me a hug. I pat her on the back. I study her for a moment. Her fingers dance and twitch like she's pushing down chords on piano keys. She seems so happy. She is drinking, of course. She likes to drink. I have no idea if she knows why I'm in Kansas City, why I'm standing here. I don't know what she knows. To my left, I see Blakey re-emerge. He pretends not to see me and walks right past us.

"Odom, are you okay?"

"Oh, fine. I'm fine."

"Enjoying the party? I can't wait to see Gavin's film."

"No, I'm not much of a party person."

"I know that."

"It's weird seeing you here. Like it's not real."

"What do you mean, Odom?"

"It feels unreal."

"Odom. This is real. I'm standing here."

"I know. I think. But usually we see each other back there."

"Right. But we're not back there."

I don't say anything back and for some reason this distresses her. She leans in closer and whispers, like everyone else is doing. "Odom. Are you okay?"

Birdshit is wearing a blue dress, cut above her knees, tightly fitted. She's wearing eye makeup and her hair has been curled. Michael approaches, she steps back. We shake hands. I tell him it's nice to see him again. My sister's hands are still twitching, making silent music. I wonder if highly skilled piano players would be able to watch her hands and interpret what chord or note she's playing, what song, what melody, like lip readers can tell what people are saying without hearing the sounds.

"So what are you doing here?" I ask.

"Driving around, seeing some of the country," Michael says. He tugs at his white shirt like he has an itch underneath it. It is heavily starched. Not only is he eighteen years younger, he's also shorter than Birdshit. By the time she was sixteen she stood almost 5'10". Michael looks to be about 5'8", but built solid. He says, "Coach, you know, I always wanted to tell you sorry."

I force an apathetic laugh. "Sorry about what? Quitting Frothmouth and transferring to Bull High School so you could play on a good team and have a shot at rushing records and scholarships and fame and glory? Just like that, forget all about where you from."

"Well, that too," he says. "But really I wanted to apologize for running the score up on y'all."

"Forgotten, Michael. I hardly remember it. Running for 548 yards and nine touchdowns. Like it never even happened."

"Coach Harrison told me to lay it on y'all and he's my coach, right? What was I to do?"

"Oh, I don't know, faked an injury, a pulled hamstring, self-inflicted ligament damage…anything would've been nice. Faked a stroke. I don't know. You could've told coach that y'all were winning sixty three to nil by halftime, no point in playing anymore. You know what, never mind. Apology accepted. Thank you, Michael."

I turn to face Birdshit. "Does Momma know where you are?"

"Not yet." She sips her drink. Diluted and brown. Probably whiskey with water.

"Gonna tell her?"

"Figured you would, now that you know where I am."

"Might be nice if you did. I think she's worried sick about you."

"I doubt that. And besides Bree knows where I am. She'll tell her. Everything is fine. Fine. It's okay. Okay? Don't worry about it."

Michael excuses himself, says he's off to go grab something to eat and asks if we want anything. Birdshit tells him to get her a plate full of pickles. He calls her sweetheart and kisses her on the cheek before walking off.

"When are you two heading back to Frothmouth?"

"I don't think we are."

"What does that mean?"

"It means that we'll probably stay here. Though nothing has been decided for sure."

"But you can't just leave… leave me."

"Odom. I can leave if I want."

"When did you decide this? And what about his probation, isn't he on probation? I thought I heard something like that? He's not even supposed to be here."

"Uncle Lou is looking into that for us."

"Oh, I see, so Uncle Lou knows about all of this? He knows everything, right? Uncle Lou knows every fucking thing."

"Odom, calm down. Knows about what?" Her eyes stare into mine, searching for clues.

"This."

"What are you talking about?"

"Going on the run, leaving town, leaving the state, coming up here."

"We aren't on the run. We're taking a vacation. Lou told us to come up here."

Blakey slaps me on the back and scares the shit out of me. I turn around and he's grinning like a noon-drunk fool. "How are my favorite brother sister pair doing?"

"We're fine." I say.

Birdshit says, "Do either of you know who that guy is?"

"Who?" We both look. "I saw him yesterday and earlier today and now he's here at this party. Seems strange. I meant to ask Lou about it but I keep forgetting."

"How's the piano playing coming along, darlin'?" Blakey says, takes a drink, ignoring her question.

"Don't play much. That guy over there, see him? In the red baseball cap?"

There he is. Mateo Panadero. He hides himself in a crowd of people when he realizes the three of us are looking at him. "How come you don't play much?" Blakey says. Then he's gone.

"Yeah," I say, thinking hard and fast. "I'm tired of this."

Lou approaches and everything stops for a moment. He slowly joins us. "Tired of what?" Lou says.

"Oh, I don't know, Lou. Someone's up to no good. You know? Someone's on our tail, following us. I think maybe I should just take care of this once and for all."

"Like what are you thinking?" Blakey says, then he eyes Lou. I motion for Lou and Blakey to step away and we walk over to a quiet spot. I lean in close so only they can hear. "What I'm saying is, Blakey, you help me go get this guy, we'll take him back to the restaurant for an interview as an investigator." I look at both of them. They're listening. "Then let me take care of the rest. I'll take him down to the basement. Get the shotgun out, put it in his face. Tell him this is one of the fringe benefits of employment. He'll shit his pants then I'll make him clean up the mess, huh?"

Lou exhales loudly, like a sigh of relief then wraps his arm around my neck playfully. "Odom, Odom, Odom. Just relax. There's no need to do anything like that, okay?"

"But, Lou," I say, my heart jumps up a gear in my chest.

"No, no. Trust me. You always trust me, don't you?"

"Of course, Lou, but..."

"Then forget about him. No need for that. Just calm down. Take a deep breath. Relax. Enjoy yourself."

Chapter Fifteen

BLAKEY AND I RIDE TOGETHER, following the caravan to Overland Park to watch the premiere. I'd asked what the damn thing was called and he couldn't remember. He sits still, balancing a bottle of Bud between his legs as he smokes. Lou is three cars ahead of us in his extra large sport utility vehicle. You can't miss the thing. It's got lights on top and on the sides, like an airplane. He's got Birdshit and Michael in there. I hope Birdshit is telling him about Mateo Panadero. Blakey takes an interest in each car that we pass or passes us—squinting through the glass trying to decipher whether Mateo Panadero is behind the wheel. "What kind of car was he driving when we saw him in Fayetteville?"

"I don't remember."

"You're a P.I. Details, right?"

"Right."

Whatever.

The seats are quickly snatched up inside the theater. I've saved the seat to my left for Blakey who said he had to use the bathroom but has been gone for twenty minutes. The tiny bass player from the band sits directly in front of me. She turns around and says hi. I wave at her but she's already turned around and doesn't see it. The lights flicker off and on; the conversations wrap up and voices get quieter, seats squeaking gently. A microphone has been set up to the left of the screen and a light shines on it and Gavin appears, coming in through the exit door. Everyone applauds. He waves with both hands.

"Thang you. Thang you. Thang you. I wanto thang allofyou fo comin," he says. I'd forgotten how he sometimes omits the last syllables of words and sometimes smashes several short words together into one.

Blakey sits down next to me.

Gavin continues, speaking slowly, articulating better, "As a documentarian of the human condition, I feel a very real responsibility to my audience..."

"Where were you?" I ask Blakey.

"Talking to Lou and Birdshit."

"About?"

Gavin's voice gets louder. His words blur in my mind as I focus on Blakey.

"Different things."

"Mateo Panadero?"

"We talked about him."

I turn back towards Gavin. Still on this human condition kick. Looks like he isn't even halfway through his remarks. He's talking about the many people he needs to thank but doesn't have time and this and that and another meaningless piece of sidebar information regarding the film. I don't much care for seeing movies at theaters. They're just so damn dark. It's the way the darkness is slowly revealed, the way lights grow dimmer and dimmer, like it's being dragged down.

Finally he says, "Any questions before we begin?"

I raise my hand, "What's this thing called again?"

"Huh?"

"I said what is the film called again?"

Gavin searches the faces in the crowd, attempting to pinpoint the direction from which my vocal has originated.

"What, what?" he says.

I stand up. "What is the name of the film?"

"Huh?"

Someone yells at me to read my ticket stub. I pull it out of my front pocket. "It's called *Sad Wings of Destiny*?"

"Huh?" Gavin is seriously lost.

"Never mind." I sit down and tell Blakey that he ripped off the title from a

Judas Priest album. Blakey tells me to shut up. The lights go out and the screen begins to display images. There is no sound. I wonder if this is a technical malfunction and sit and wait. I turn around and look up at the projection window, and notice the dust and particles floating in the air, illuminated by the beam shooting from the projector. It's still quiet. On the screen there are only shots of bands, faces, instruments, stages, Los Angeles, etc. No one else seems to be concerned.

Just as I'm about to drop my eyelids for a snooze, a loud bang of guitars roars on both sides of me. It sounds like 7th graders practicing Van Halen songs on their out of tune Ibanez guitars, pulling on the whammy bar as hard as they can. The voiceover states, "This is Los Angeles 1988, the world has never seen anything like it, boys dressed like girls… what happens," the voice asks the audience, "when your dreams are never realized? What happens to you? How do you survive? Where do the dreams go to die? And most importantly, where are you today?" This cuts into a montage of three and four second clips of bands, singers, guitar players, groupies, venues and then stops on one particular fool named Ace of Aces. He's the lead singer, or was the lead singer of a band called Ambition. The screen splits, Ace of Aces then, 1988. Ace of Aces today, he's in prisoner orange. I really don't care and close my eyes again and keep them closed throughout the barrage of noise and voices until I hear clapping and I figure it's over.

Gavin steps up to the microphone.

"Any questions?"

No one dares.

The post-premiere shindig is at a sponsor's suburban McMansion. It's way out in the middle of nowhere, the most southern edge of the metropolitan area on 198th St. or some ridiculous white-flight address. The conversation fodder is identical: plumbing and insects. The host put up an undisclosed sum to help push Gavin's film into production and helped to support the marketing budget which includes several showings, another one in Kansas City, one in Lawrence. They're trying desperately to set up something in Omaha and Des Moines. In the first five minutes several Overland Park locals approach me with one hand stretched for an introductory shake, the other fondling a dozen business cards, ready to dispense. "Hi, this is great, isn't it? I'm in sales. What do you do?" I'd say, "Nothing." "You look familiar," a thirtyish woman said, and then before she could make a guess or substantiate her opening, said, "I'm Kathy. I'm a Business Client Coordinator. I'm a liaison between business clients who want…" she rambled. I felt a hint of stomach acid crawl back up my esophagus. One man boldly handed me his business card, then winked and said, "Need advertising. Call me." He punctuated his sales pitch by pointing forcefully at the card he'd handed me. I let go of it and it floated, slowly to the ground.

I remember SportsCenter and ask this guy standing next to me what time it is. He makes a big deal about having to pull his cell phone out of his jacket pocket to tell me. It's 11:45. I missed it.

Blakey and Trisha have resumed their courtship. At times they hold hands; often he wraps his arm around her waist. Every ten minutes Luke comes by and asks if everything is okay. The tiny bass player is here, talking to her drummer. I'm ready to go back to Frothmouth and be done with this whole thing.

There's a tap on my shoulder. Of course when I turn to the side the tap came from there is no one there. I turn the other way and see Birdshit giggling herself into a fit. "It amazes me that people still fall for that." She laughs so hard she begins to have trouble breathing. I worry an asthma attack is about to begin. An attack that will probably lead to an emergency room visit and three armloads full of ephedrine and a misty mask taped around her face, inhaling the medicated vapors. We've been through this so many times. "You okay?"

"Fine," she says, sucking in deep breaths, then pausing to see if indeed she is fine.

"Where's Michael?"

"He's around."

"What did you think of the film?"

"I thought it was a film."

"Well, that's a fair critique."

"I don't."

"Still writing poetry?"

"In fact I am. Water Dribble Press is publishing volume two at the end of the year."

"*Still Lost*?"

"That's the one."

"Congratulations. Are you going on a reading tour?"

"I doubt it. No one reads poetry."

"Only people who write it."

"Pretty much."

"How is Momma doing?"

"She's okay. You haven't stopped by in awhile."

"I know. It's been a few months."

"It's been six months, Odom. Don't think Momma doesn't know better. Six months is a long time not to visit, especially considering that she lives three miles away."

"I know it. So you're doing okay?"

"I'm more than okay. I'm in love. Michael is a sweetheart. He treats me so well."

"This is a serious thing you got going."

"More serious than anything I've been involved in before." This sounds familiar. I'm less than convinced and can't think of anything to say, so we stand there looking at one another.

The tiny bass player interrupts us. She apologizes. Birdshit melts into the crowd of suits.

"Who are you?" I ask.

"I'm Amber."

"The tiny bass player Amber?"

"Never been called the tiny bass player before."

"I've never had a girl follow me around for an entire night."

This triggers a memory and my thoughts immediately go to Bree. I followed her around our town's dirt roads without her knowing about it for a few weeks, or maybe it was a month or longer, before I made my move. It was easy and destined, like things tend to be in small towns. I wonder what would happen if I got to know Amber a little better. What would I say if she asked me questions? I imagine I'd tell her the truth. Strangers can bring that out in a way you're not prepared for. Amber is still standing there. "What did you think of the film?" She scrunches up her lips on one side and looks off to her right, in deep thought. It's the least attractive she's looked all night. "Hmmm."

"You don't have to give me an academic answer," I say.

"Well. I liked it. But I think it could've been better."

"That's pretty much what I thought."

"What is your name? I feel so silly asking you."

"That's okay. My name is Odom. Odom Shiloh."

"Odom? I've never met an Odom before."

"I've known a few Ambers. You're the first Amber I liked."

"I guess I'll take that as a compliment."

"Sure. If you want."

"Odom, can I ask you a personal question?"

"I'd probably better say yes."

"Why do you wear a wedding ring? I talked to that bald guy over there that is always with you and he said you're not really married. That you're in the process of a divorce but you still live with your wife or ex-wife?"

"Something like that."

"I'm sorry. It's none of my business. I mean, I guess I made it my business by asking that bald guy."

"His name is Blakey."

"That's right. But I guess I'm kind of glad I'm making it my business. Does that make any sense? Probably not."

"It makes sense."

"So how come you wear the wedding ring?"

"I wear it, I guess," I say, glancing down at my hand, "because I still feel responsible for her in a way. I have to take care of her. Not sure how long that feeling will last though. She's never really had anyone who genuinely cares about her. Don't get me wrong, she's a pain in the ass. But without me, she won't have anyone else."

Amber listens attentively. This is what a girl will do when she is interested: ask questions and listen. I continue, "For as different as we are, she's a lot like me. She's one of us. That's kind of a long explanation for such an easy question. I guess I could've just said something like, I never had a reason to take it off."

"Do you think you'll have a reason to take it off?"

"I don't know. A very wise man, my father actually, once told me that you never know what you're capable of until it's too late."

"Very wise indeed."

"He was the smartest man I've ever known. Blakey comes in a close second but my father has him beat by a mile. Before you ask, I will tell you that he's no longer around and I honestly don't know if he's dead or if he's just gone off somewhere. I don't know if I'll ever see him again. I doubt I will. But I can't help it, sometimes I imagine a reunion with him."

"That's got to be tough."

"Everything is tough sometimes. That's something else he'd tell me. Nothing is easy. Even the best things in life are tough sometimes. I doubt he ever tasted any of the best things in life. I don't know if that makes sense or sounds kind of dumb but I think it's true. He was a strange man."

"Sounds like it."

"Know what else he said? He said not to bother trying to figure things out, that nothing makes sense and it never will. I think that's probably good advice. But sometimes he would say things that made no sense, even speaking in languages I'd never heard of or ones he'd made up. That wasn't very often though."

I gaze at this open space about ten yards away. Birdshit is standing on the left and is surrounded by a group of people. To the right of this space is the end of a couch. And I'm being sucked into this space by something powerful, like a memory. But I can't figure it out.

I feel like I've unlocked something; like I've stumbled into a room I didn't mean to enter but once there I realize it's where I wanted to be all along. It feels familiar but it's cold and dusty. It's been a long time. My immediate reaction is to turn around and run. But I can't; I'm drawn to wreckage all around me.

Luke breaks my concentration by sitting on the couch and putting a pickle in his mouth. He gives me a peculiar look.

"Let's go sit down somewhere," Amber says.

"Okay."

Amber and I go outside and sit on the back deck. As we do I see people covering their mouths and lowering their voices as I walk by. Some are whispering. It feels like everybody is whispering.

The deck is top rate, a deck that looks rarely used. There's one of those enormous, top-dollar grills that is electronic and programmable and imposing. That's why you buy these things, because they look imposing. I doubt a hot dog or hamburger patty has ever been delicately placed atop the artificial coals that heat up this stainless steel jobber that was manufactured in some small southern town whose pride rests solely on the production of these giant, glorified microwaves. Amber smokes just like Blakey, inhaling a good part of the stick in a drag. "I quit these things before but I started again last year."

"How come? I thought when you quit something that's it."

"I'm not sure. It doesn't take much to get started again. This is nice out here."

"I have the feeling we're the very first inhabitants."

She amuses herself into a soulful smokers hack. It's unsettling to bear witness to. Her voice downshifting to a deep reverberation of a testosterone-rich elderly gentlemen. "You okay?"

"Fine," she says, wiping something from her mouth onto the back of her hand. Then she casually massages it into her jeans until a damp residue is left. She spins the little wheel on her lighter.

"So you're a professional musician?"

"Professional enough, I suppose. I get paid if that's what you're asking."

"You have a pretty voice. It kinda goes with everything else about you."

"Are you being sweet or just losing track of your words?"

"Huh?"

"You don't drink much do you?"

"Not really."

She drinks from her Bud bottle.

"Want to go back inside?"

"Okay."

I excuse myself from Amber's view and grab Blakey by his arm and pull him aside, down the end of a deserted hallway with no lights. He stands in front of me in the darkness awaiting the urgent message I am loaded to deliver. He's a little drunk and pinches an unlit cigarette between his thumb and forefinger.

"What are we doing, Blakey?"

"I don't know what you're doing but I'm discussing this wonderful documentary. I'm having a great time splicing and dicing it. A group of us are brainstorming and coming up with some suggestions, maybe some last minute edits to help make the narrative arc more natural. A lot of it feels a little forced right now.

Uneven, a little too front-heavy and not enough at the end. But with a few more of the right moves, it could be the five-minute love-child that Sophia Coppola and David Lynch conceived during intermission at the drive-in movie. Do you gather that as well?"

"What I mean is, what are we doing here? What is going on? What's all the whispering about? Why is everyone looking at me? When do we go home? Birdshit has been found and seems to be going nowhere. So what now? I'm not paying you to socialize at parties."

"I'm retiring. I told you that. Blakey Flake's Intimiate Resolutions is closed for business; the Bald Eagle is migrating north. You're on your own. I'm probably going to hang out here for a few days, maybe a week. Got me a pretty girl that says I can stay with her if I like."

"Okay."

"How's the little dark haired number that's been following you around like a lost puppy? Someone you need to introduce me to?"

"Okay," I mumble, examining my hands. "I'm driving back to Frothmouth tomorrow morning. Am I driving down by myself?"

Blakey smoothes out his shirt over his concave stomach. "Looks that way. I'm not sure why you don't just stay here too, at least for a few days or a week or so. Lou's got guest rooms at his house. Or stay with Luke or Gavin. There's not a whole lot waiting for you down in Frothmouth."

"It's home, Blakey."

"So what? You need to leave it behind."

"Okay."

About the time I give up on the darkness of the hallway and begin my journey back to the light, a figure appears at the end of the hallway. From the short distance between the two of us, I have trouble identifying the image. It comes closer, moving very slowly, and eventually I see the massive stature and white hair flipped over the top and I realize that it's Lou.

"Going somewhere?" Lou's voice is low, soft and clear.

"Not necessarily. Enjoying the party?"

"I've never been much of a party person. But I'm here. You know why I'm here?"

"Because you were invited?"

"Because you are here and because Birdshit is here. I have to watch out for you two like I always have."

"Well, you know you don't have to worry about me. Now it never hurts to have an extra set of eyes on my sister."

"And on you too. How's that step-son of yours?"

"Fine. Bree's homeschooling him, so I'm sure he'll end up sorting through dumpsters for a living."

"You sound angry."

"No, I'm not. I'm fine. I never get angry. Except sometimes Blakey can get on my nerves."

"I've seen you angry before."

"Yeah? So what?"

"What's going to happen to you, Odom?"

"What do you mean?"

"With everything going on the way it is. Your second marriage down the drain."

"How do you know about that?"

"People call me. I answer. They tell me things. I listen."

"Well, it doesn't bother me."

"I'm more worried about you than I am about your sister. She seems to be getting things together. I'm not so sure about you."

"Talk to me in a month about how well Birdshit is getting things together." I laugh, look down at my feet and kick my toe into the carpet.

"I'm still not so sure about you."

"I'm just going through a tough time."

"I think things are about to get tougher."

"Says who?"

"Says me."

"How come?"

"There's a lot you need to know. Things to learn."

"Really? What do I need to know?"

"For starters, there is no secret basement."

I take two steps closer to him, lower my voice and test it. "Lou." It's too loud. I lower it even more, almost to a whisper. "Lou. Can you hear me?"

"Yes, Odom, I can," he whispers back. I watch the shape of his lips create the words and let them go. "What is it?"

"I *know* about the secret basement. It's okay."

"Odom. There is no other way to say it. There is no secret basement. I'll show you. It's full of soda syrups. There's a freezer down there where we store the meat."

"My daddy, your brother, told me about the basement. It's been a secret place for a long time. Where you all meet. The Shiloh's. Why would he tell me about it if it doesn't exist?"

"Your daddy said a lot of things that weren't true."

I'm not shocked by this. In fact, I know it. I study Lou's face. It's sincere. "Like what?"

"About the basement and these other alleged secrets. I think the only secrets that exist are the ones between you and him."

"I don't know what you're talking about. I think I'm going to just get out of your way and head back down to Arkansas tonight. Maybe I'll stop in Joplin or Fayetteville and stay the night and get back to Frothmouth by early afternoon tomorrow. Bree needs me and that asshole step-son of mine needs me, too. Yeah. I just need to get out of here. I knew I shouldn't have come. Glad everyone is happy. Everyone except me."

I force my hands into my pockets, feeling for my car keys with my right hand, loop them around my index finger and pull them out like a fishing hook.

"Odom. You might not want to get on back there so soon."

"Why wouldn't I?"

"That bicyclist that got hit by that car in Memphis. He died this evening."

TWO

Chapter Sixteen

I DIDN'T GIVE LOU an opportunity to elaborate on his comments. Obviously there's something going on behind my back that I've been unaware of. Bree probably called Lou and told him about the police showing up. And Birdshit called Lou and said she and Michael were on their way to Kansas City and needed a place to hide out and start over. I don't know anymore. It hurts my head to think about the possibilities. Maybe that's where insanity begins: when everywhere you stretch to try to feel your way back you can't feel anything. Except the impression that it just keeps going.

When I get back to my hotel room I double-check the phone—still unplugged—and turn on the television, clicking through the channels looking for ESPN or any news show that might bother mentioning the death of a French cyclist. The room is pristinely clean. Blakey's ashtray has been shaved of its filtered Medusa hair and given a scrub-down. The sixty-some odd cents in change I'd left inside the ashtray by the sink has been lifted. A blatant theft. Of course, the room attendant would argue in court that they mistook the sixty-some odd cents in change as a tip. I wonder how much these petty thieves can earn doing this kind of dirty work.

That's him! I turn up the volume on the television. "...died this morning, the result of injuries suffered at last week's Memphis 300 bike race. Police are saying that they are very close to making an arrest in the case. As you may recall, Pierre collided with a motorist in downtown Memphis...."

How does Lou know. Is he in on this investigation. How in the world is this happening. Why now. How can he just die like that. How can that happen. When will they pick me up. There's no way. I don't get it. He died. How can that happen. He's dead. I'll go to court, to trial and they'll find me guilty of something, no doubt. What do they charge people with who they can't nab for first-degree murder? Aggravated manslaughter? Third-degree murder? I'm a dead man too.

Me and Pierre are both dead men.

Even if I have doubts, I can't let them in.

What do I say when they drag me in for questioning and tell me the prosecutor will be going for the death penalty. They'll ask about my father and probably tag me for crimes he committed. Can't find the father, charge the son. Crimes of the father. Or sins of the father. Whatever the Bible said. Punitive damages. I never read the Bible. Daddy said not to. Said the Bible is junk. Said that the gods live underground. That crazy son of a bitch said a lot of things.

One of the last things I remember him working on was building an underground bunker, out behind our house. Daddy had said this was his way of obtaining eternal life. To live down there with them. Heaven is downward, not upwards, he'd laugh. He screamed and pointed at the clouds. All these fools think that's where they're going.

He lived in a shed behind the house. He'd moved out there shortly after Birdshit was born. He didn't take too well to her. It got to where I was the only contact between him and Momma. I was sent out to his shed. Its construction was less than sound. Several strong storms blew portions of it away, leaving him to desperately nail new pieces of lumber across the holes to keep the rain out. He never came back into the house anymore. He did all his dirty work out in the woods. The nature of business.

I took him his food. I took him any notes or important things he needed to know about. Momma handed me bottles of whiskey and vodka and gin to give him, or stacked cardboard boxes full of Old Milwaukee on my outstretched arms. It quiets him, she'd say. If he don't get his drink, he goes crazy. But sometimes he'd drink too much and go crazy the other way. It's when things were evenly balanced in the middle and his eyes sparkled from the alcohol soaking his brain that he'd talk to me, tell me stories about car rides we went on, places we'd gone together. Secret places. Places and rides I didn't remember too well at first. He always had a way of finding a clue that opened the door in my mind; suddenly I'd see everything all over again, up there on my mind's own stage.

Our old dog Butter used to sleep just outside the shed. Daddy didn't like him to be inside the shed with him. So Butter made his home right outside the door. When it would thunder and storm or if it got to be too cold, Butter would bark without stopping. This troubled Daddy so much that he finally had to put Butter to sleep. It was more of a nightmare for Butter. Daddy did it himself, shooting Butter's face off with his old shotgun that stood in the corner of his shed, next to the cot he slept on.

We called him Butter because one time when he was still a young pup, he managed to get up on the table and burrow his face into a mixing bowl that had five cups of butter sliding down the side of it. Momma was fixin' to make cookies and cakes and little Butter had gotten up there and was lapping up the creamy taste. Butter was the last dog we had. The only one I remember. I remember Daddy shooting Butter's face off. He did it without even warning me. He just went inside, got the gun, aimed it and pulled the trigger. It happened so fast my mind had to stop and rewind for a second and put everything back in the proper order and make sure I had indeed seen what I did just see. Daddy made me pick up Butter by the tail and drop the back half of him into a Hefty bag. I didn't much feel like picking up the three pieces that were left of his face so I knelt down and held open another Hefty bag and kicked the pieces into it and then put both bags inside another Hefty bag, twisted it, tied it and then wrapped a few of those little twisty-ties around it for good measure. Then I carried the pieces to the woods and buried Butter.

Daddy never did get that underground bunker completely dug out. He moved a lot of dirt and once in a while stared down at it but it never seemed to be enough. After he left, Momma paid David Garner to dump a load of dirt in the hole. She also had David destroy the shed. I remember David sitting with a bottle of Old Crow, watching the boards and shingles burn. All that remains now is a scorched patch of dirt and those woods behind them, still sulking in wait.

The same woods where Daddy taught me my first real lessons. The time he walked with me for half a day deep into them, and then during a break in which we bit into ham and mustard sandwiches on white bread, he handed me a pill and told me to take it. He said it would give me strength. I was tired at that point. The next thing I knew I was waking up and it was dark and I was alone. It took me two days to find my way out of those woods. He thought it had taken me about a day and half too long to find my way home. This outdoors stuff didn't come naturally to me at first, firing guns, killing and growing food, all of that was hard. But he taught me to survive, said that the Shiloh's could survive anything because when the chips were down we could retreat into the woods, disappear and stay alive.

In the woods.

It was his place, then our place and now it is mine.

I hadn't been back deep into those woods since he disappeared. Part of me thinks that's where he is; that he's been living out there for all these years. He's there somewhere. I know it. He had to have just walked into them and that was it. The woods carry on for about twenty miles eastwardly until they hit rice fields and flatten out. Between those rice fields and the back of our house, is where he has to be.

I have to find him and ask him if all of those secrets he shared were real.

I turn the television off, pull the covers over my face and fall asleep.

The phone rings, waking me up with a start. I grab the phone. "THIS IS YOUR WAKE-UP CALL. THIS IS YOUR WAKE-UP CALL. THIS IS YOUR WAKE-UP CALL."

I thought the phone was unplugged.

I unplug the phone.

I check out and drive back to Arkansas.

Chapter Seventeen

THE WATER FEELS very cool as I settle into it, leaning my head back, wetting my hair. My stomach feels tight and knotted like I haven't eaten in several days. My eyes are electric with exhaustion but the sight of water left me no option. I had to get in.

I have always loved the water.

I long ago discovered my favorite place to be is underwater.

There was a time when Birdshit, Momma and I ended up in Florida. We were running from something. What we were running from was kept a secret. I don't remember the name of the hotel we stayed in, but it was white and sat on a beautiful stretch of beach and we stayed there for a while, a few weeks, maybe even a month.

The ocean was only a fifty-yard walk from our room, separated by a sliding glass door. Every morning, every afternoon and every evening we went out to the water, the three of us. Momma lathered us in a permanent layer of white sunscreen lotion and red, plastic sunglasses to protect our eyes from the relentless sunlight.

Momma would lead us out into the water very slowly. I felt I was old enough and a strong enough swimmer to venture out on my own, but she never allowed me this privilege beyond splashing about in water calf high. We'd go into the water, Momma floating on her back, Birdshit hanging onto her arm and me a few yards off diving head first into the water, reaching for the bottom with my hands, sticking my gangly legs above the surface, wobbling them in the air. I'd hold my breath and see how long I could stay below. I fell in love with the silence around me, the serene stillness of the underworld—experiencing an awareness about myself that felt more real than anything on dry land. A world it seemed, that only I existed in. I was living down there and I never wanted to go back up to the surface, I wanted to stay below. I almost did once, trying so hard not to go back up, with blackness creeping around the edges of my eyesight, darkness rocking me slowly to sleep and just when I thought this was all there was, I saw Momma reach down for me, coming down to me, grabbing me by the elbow and pulling me up, back to their world. "Breathe!" she yelled at me. I coughed and sucked in air. "Momma, I'm okay," I assured her. "Why were you down there so long? Don't do that, you scare me when you do that."

"I like it down there, Momma."

And so I went, down below the world's surface. I spent almost all my time on that trip diving in and out of the water, sucking in deep breaths and holding it until I felt like I was about to let go.

Chapter Eighteen

I'M CROSSING OVER into Arkansas and stop off in Fayetteville to get gas and lunch. I take my time navigating through the town. I haven't spent much time in Fayetteville. It's where everyone in the state seems to want to migrate. In the old days, Fayetteville was an isolated little college town on top of a small mountain. Today it's something else entirely. I don't recognize it. It doesn't look the same as I remember thirty years ago when I'd come up here for football games with the Fergusons. The people look fancier, more delicate. They're shinier and polished and they all drive cars that look part luxury sedan, part rocket ship. The occasional green Chevrolet pickup hums by with an elderly gentleman driving, or a high school kid with his sleeves rolled up and a well-worn ball cap set straight around his head.

I cut through the University of Arkansas campus, noticing that the stadium looks twice the size it used to be. I keep driving, turning right, going up a hill into the heart of campus. It's hard to believe that most of these kids are twenty years younger than I am. To think how lucky they are, in school, their entire lives waiting for them outside this place when they're ready.

I wonder where these kids come from. Small towns? Out of state? I turn again and follow the flow of traffic, going where most of the cars go. I pass several fraternity houses and watch the boys with unkempt hair and two days of face stubble push and shove and kid in their designer khakis. The sons of Little Rock businessmen, south Arkansas oil families, wherever it is people like this come from. I didn't grow up with these kinds of folks. I have no idea what I would say to them.

When I was in my late teens I wanted to go to school here. But Momma said I needed to stay close. So I went to Jonesboro and after a year I quit. I was driving home every weekend anyhow. No point in pretending I was getting an education when I had to take care of things back home. The money we had meant I didn't have to work. That's all Momma would say, that we got money, don't sweat an education. It don't matter, she said. I got a house paid for and enough money to pay my bills until the age of 178 if I were to live that long. That's what money means to me. Not some chance to create a bigger version of myself with the fancy bows and trimmings. I don't need a rocket ship, I just need a roof.

In the rearview I see a cop behind me about thirty yards back. I'm hoping he turns off before I hit this light ahead of me, which is red. The cop pulls right in behind me. We are stopped. I glance at my rearview. The cop is a man, older, with cop shades on. He doesn't appear to be paying me much attention. He's not on the radio or looking down to his right, where the cop computers are, where he'd be punching in my license plate number. I hope not, at least. I'm really not that nervous. I know that 95% of being a cop is blowing smoke and pretending to know things that you don't. That's their angle. So to hear on the television that the police are very near making an arrest is so much bullshit; any third grader can see through that cloud of cop smoke. It means they don't have shit. If they had a serious person of interest, they would not be announcing it. They would have already arrested the person. That person being me.

The light turns green. I want to turn left but realize my blinker is not on and figure it'd be too hasty to flip it on for a half second before making the turn. That would certainly result in a ticket and cop lecture about the dangers of careless driving. The car ahead of me turns left, no blinker of course. I go straight. So does the cop. Then I see the lights flashing and two quick toots on his cop siren. Not the whining siren we see in movies. Out here things are never the way they are in the movies.

Okay. I pull over immediately at an awkward angle, almost entirely blocking the lane of traffic. The cop stops and gets out of the car. I don't buy it. There's no way. I roll down my window and wait.

"Hello there," the cop says. I thumb through my wallet, flipping through business cards.

"Hi. How are you doing?" The cards start to fall out of my hand into my lap, onto the floorboard.

"Good. Can you keep your hands where I can see them."

Okay. I put my hands in my lap and stare at them.

"Good. Wanted to make sure you didn't have any weapons. Now, can I see your license and proof of insurance?"

I manage to pry my license from the see-thru visor on the front of my wallet and pull out my insurance card, a crumbling piece of cheap business card paper, the edges rounded smooth, the ink fading. I manage to see that it's still valid, through the end of the month, three more weeks. I had lost track of when it expired. I always pay the entire year in one payment, leaving it to the insurance company to remind me when I need to send them more money. They never forget to remind me.

He takes them, peeks down at my license, seems to be studying the picture, doing several back and forth gestures with his eyes between the license picture and me. "Did you know that your license plate is expired?"

"No, I didn't." I turn around instinctively, assuming I can clearly see the error from the front seat of my car.

"Today is the seventh of the month, expired seven days ago."

"Damn." I smack my head with my palm and mumble to myself, just loud enough for him to hear, "I told myself last week to get this taken care of but Bree had to go to the emergency room and I forgot and I don't know. I can't believe this." Then I fully realize what he's said. It's the seventh of the month? I thought it was the third or fourth? That cop in Louisiana didn't mention anything about expired plates.

"Is that plate the proper plate for this vehicle?"

"What do you mean?"

"I mean, if I call in this license plate number will it come back saying it belongs to," he reads my license, "an Odom Shiloh and the car is a Honda, green, four door, a..." he does a left to right sweep of the car trying to make a guess at something.

"Of the year 1997," I say, "and yessir, that's what the record will show."

"Now, do I need to go do that or can I trust you?"

"You can trust me."

"Now why is that?"

"Because an honest man never tells a lie."

He smiles and looks up, something up there holding his attention. He says, "You know what the difference between telling the truth and lie is?"

I rub my hands on the tops of my legs, suddenly nervous. "No, sir. I don't believe I do. I mean, I wouldn't know the difference being that I'm the kind that doesn't take to lying."

"A lie is something you have to remember. The truth remembers itself."

"Yessir," I say, completely confused and doubting myself, nearing a mental panic.

"You okay?"

"Yessir. Why you ask?"

"You just kinda got all nervous and your face is red as a beet."

"A what?"

"A beet. You can wipe your brow there, looks like it's nearing flood level."

"Yessir," I say, raising my forearm and swiping it across my face. Several drops of perspiration fall into my lap. My arm is moist.

"Take a deep breath."

"Okay." I inhale deeply.

"Now, hold it."

"I'm sorry?"

"You just messed it up. Take in a deep breath and hold it in. Don't exhale until I tell you so."

I inhale deeply like a doctor has a stethoscope on my back listening for pneumonia or bronchitis. I hold it for many seconds, almost a minute, eyeing the officer.

He nods. "Now, exhale." He watches me. "Feel okay now?"

"Definitely okay now."

Several awkward seconds pass. "Very well then. Consider this a warning and get this taken care of. I can tell you that the next police officer that pulls you over ain't gonna be so sweet on you like me."

"Yessir."

"I'm sweet because I'm getting older. Old age makes you chew a little slower."

"Yessir."

As I pull out I make a mental note to get those tags paid as soon as possible. I must have overlooked the notice in the mail or else Bree has been getting sloppy with the mail or purposely throwing it out. Now that I think about it, it seems like forever ago that I mailed Visa a payment or paid the water and electric. I bet she is doing that on purpose. She's probably moving out right now. I'll get home and the lights won't work, water won't pour from the faucets, there'll be nothing but magazines for me. I'll head to the shitter with another swimsuit issue and get stuck with my own shit when I jiggle the handle.

There was zero fuss from her when I informed Bree that I was leaving to go fetch Birdshit. In the past she'd hissy-fit over a trip to the post office or a jaunt down the road to Garner's without her. It can only mean that she's found someone else. I don't believe you can make someone love you or love you again once they've given up. Love takes over you like sleep and then you wake up.

I should have known this is how it would end: no confrontation, no working things out. The accumulation of sadness and the non-payment of bills. I did know this would happen. It's true she's beautiful and always will be. And she'll marry many more. I'm just one in a chain.

She can go run off and take that kid of hers with her. The only poor son of a bitch named Sparkman in the history of the world and two nicknames to that: Spark and Sparky. She had that kid when she was in the eighth grade. Bree was so darn pretty that the most handsome man in Dallas County took away what wasn't his. Took it away when he was supposed to be watching over her, protecting her from the very evil that he felt only Jesus could combat.

She'd been raised by law-abiding and god-fearing type parents. She was thirteen at the time and by herself for the night. Her parents had gone down to Smackover to attend a funeral and asked Marty Shortledge to stop by, visit with her and make sure things were all right. Bree knew how to fire a shotgun and her father had set it up next to the fireplace for her, loaded and ready to take down any intruder that might test his luck.

Marty Shortledge was forty-one years old, a handsome and fit man who was tanned and strong from working his farm in Pine Grove. He owned three dealerships selling trucks, ATV's and the like. The people in the surrounding towns looked up to him. He had a cross tattooed on his right forearm and did a lot of lip service to the ideas of right and wrong. Everything was that simple for him; either right or wrong, black or white, Jesus or the Devil, and always remembering the good Lord's forgiveness in all choices bad.

What he did to Bree was wrong, an all out assault. There was no sweetness or lure. He didn't warm her up with jokes and cans of beer. He walked into that house after her parents had plenty good and long time to get where they were going and pulled Bree to him with his greasy right hand wrapped around the back of her neck so hard she felt paralyzed and started pulling off her clothes with his left hand, going back and forth between her and unbuttoning his Wranglers. Bree told me that at the beginning of the attack, she looked at that shotgun good and hard, thinking of a way to stop him momentarily—a promise to undress herself—enough of an opening to allow her to reach over and put the shotgun to his face. She said that's what she tried to focus on the entire time he was hitting her and hurting her so bad she felt like she wasn't even there, just a pair of eyes staring at a gun leaning against the fireplace.

Marty is something she's only told me about, she says. And every once in awhile she'll say, "Do you think I should've killed Marty Shortledge?" And every time I say, "Yes." And she still asks me even though she knows my answer will never change, and because she knows now that her answer then won't ever change what she wishes she'd done. Waiting to see if I'll change my answer because she can't change hers.

Chapter Nineteen

THE HONDA CARRIES ME further south, up and down the hills along I-540 between Fayetteville and Fort Smith. This has to be one of the most beautiful stretches of road in the country, and no one knows about it. The hills so massive and overpowering you feel outmatched. I come to a long bridge that serves as the link between the edges of a huge canyon; for hundreds of yards below the bridge there is nothing. Driving over it I imagine what would happen if my Honda and I sailed off the bridge downward into the trees and forest; it would be very possible no one would ever find me. Like those explorers who go into the Amazon rainforests and are never heard from again. What a beautiful way to disappear. I wonder what it'd feel like to disappear.

Every so often I see a lone cabin or small house atop one of the serene hills of the Ozarks and think how lucky they must be to live up there. A windmill turning. Water from a well. Live on top of everything. To step outside your home and see trees and air and openness. This must be what hope feels like, living on top of one of those hills. I let several cars roar past me; two of them appear to be racing as they take turns pulling ahead, cutting each other off. I let off the gas in anticipation of a major catastrophic accident—one of these bozos clipping the other's back fender, sending it into a spin, taking out several cars and forcing other cars to launch airborne and crashing into the side of the hills. The slower speed feels better. I'm not in a hurry.

I pull off at Alma to use the bathroom and top off the tank. Half a dozen locals sit around tables inside the gas station. Two little kids pick up packages of candy, look them over and place them back on the shelf in the wrong spots. It's a miniature grocery store and there's a restaurant inside the place. I stand outside the Men's bathroom and wait because the door is locked. After several minutes pass I begin to wonder if anyone is inside. I try the door again; it's still locked. The door to the Women's is wide open. It's one of those one-at-a-time bathrooms. I look around and close the Women's door behind me, lift up the toilet lid and force the piss out of me. I push with all my might, the piss coming out of me at close to a hundred miles an hour. They say that's how fast a sneeze is but I can't figure how or why anyone took the time to figure that out. I shake it, zip it and open the door hoping like you wouldn't believe that's there's no little lady standing outside. I didn't hear the door jiggle. That's a good sign.

I emerge, my eyes wildly searching my immediate environment, and find no awaiting female bathroom seekers. I tug on the Men's bathroom door again out of curiosity. It's still locked. Then I see the table of locals looking right at me. I failed to notice the angle they had on the bathrooms from their position. They saw me go in the Women's. I know they have it in for me. If I were in Atlanta or Chicago no one would even care. Not here. Someone will say something, I just know it. I walk past then cut left over to the coolers and study the beverage options. I hear one of them say, "That just ain't right." Someone else agrees and says loud enough so I can hear that there's a reason they have signs on them. The 16-ounce bottles are on sale and I grab one, an orange flavor and stand in line. I pay with cash and thank the attendant behind the counter.

She says, "Sir, I can ring you up over here."

I turn around and two Mexicans place their sodas and bags of chips on the counter. She starts punching them in, the machine making a beeping sound in between items.

The woman says, "Are all of these together or separate?"

The Mexicans, two guys that look to be nineteen or twenty and dressed in work boots, jeans and green shirts, both point to the items with their fingers.

"I said, do you want me to ring these up together?"

I turn around and say to the closest one, "Estan separados o juntos?"

"Separados," he says.

I tell her that they're separate.

"Don't tell me you're one of them too."

"One of what?"

"These Hispanics."

"No, I'm not Hispanic."

"Sound like it. Can't get a job much anymore unless you speak a foreign language. A shame, ain't it? About the only jobs left are working at Wal-Mart."

The woman does her finger dancing with the register, totaling up the orders. They both thank me in Spanish. "Ningún problema. Tener un buen día. Adios," I say and leave.

I get on I-40 headed towards Little Rock. I forgot about the gas. I don't need it. I can wait until Little Rock. The only class I cared much for in high school and that one year of college was Spanish. I couldn't think of anything more exciting than speaking a language that was not your own. I thought about going to Mexico and waking up in a cloud of bordello smoke. I thought about a lot of things then.

I can't think of what I'm going to say to Bree when I get home. I'll probably do the listening. I'm confident she's rehearsing her big speech right now, standing in front of a mirror or even practicing it out on Sparkman. He'll sit there, blinking, while she recites her tirade, saying, "I hate you. I never loved you. You been bad to my son, been bad to me, been bad to yourself, Odom Shiloh."

The poor kid has always been her partner in crime. When he was a baby Bree's parents gave her the boot; any child born out of wedlock was a child of sin. While she was first on her own she'd stuff packages of chicken breasts and pork chops into his diaper. She'd take empty baby bottles in the store, take apple juice off the shelf, fill up the bottles and stroll away. She's crooked just like her smile. The straight life isn't for her. She met me thinking this is how things are supposed to be. A house on a large bit of land, quiet nights, sitting on the porch, chatting, gossiping and watching the wind blow through the woods, guessing at what our neighbors were up to when they drove past the bumpy road we all shared. I've known for a while she wasn't all that pleased with her choice. Being pretty in a small town don't bring much in the way of excitement. In a big city like Nashville or New Orleans, hell, every day could be just that day you'd read about, dreamed about and always wanted. There are possibilities. She wants those possibilities, not commitments. I guess all women do.

It occurs to me that all things considered, my best option may be to drive straight to Memphis and turn myself in. I could demonstrate psychological inconsistency or detachment. Who knows. They might let me off. In my mind it plays out as a noble act, taking responsibility, doing my time, paying my fines, mouthing quotable exclamations of remorse. Maybe give this Jesus Christ crap a go. Turn my life over to him for a few weeks and see what comes of it. If nothing does, I can put him back where he belongs.

But really. Fuck that. I don't want to go to jail or prison if I can avoid it. Honesty would probably garner me a longer sentence. If I stood up before the judge and said, "I'm guilty. I take full responsibility," they'd give me the maximum sentence plus some. Mayor Ferguson says that all prosecutors are crooks. But if I get me an attorney who stands up for me and says, "Your honor, this has been a huge misunderstanding. My client may be guilty, he may not be, but I'm sure we can work out something that is amicable and fair." In other words, you shut up and let someone else speak for you. Then I can count on doing the least amount of time without having to 'fess up to anything. That's what you're paying for, the luxury of not having to talk. It's a funny message to try and tell people the world doesn't work that way. My daddy did always say that the biggest confusion we all suffer from is this inability to discern the real world from the one we create in our own heads. And he wasn't talking about your monkey-eyed crazies and bona fide wackos who talk to trees and make sculptures out of their own shit. Maybe I could catch a break the way Blakey got himself cleared down in Shreveport.

My thoughts quickly turn to Momma and my need to have a sit-down with her. It's been months, as Birdshit reminded me. It's strange. I never thought of it until recently but imagine all those years when Daddy was living out there in the woods and she couldn't even talk to him.

The driving becomes more monotonous. I'm bored. I decide to stay the night in Little Rock. It'll only be late afternoon by the time I get into town. I need some time to myself before Frothmouth. I pull out my cell phone. I have eight missed calls. I'll check them later. They can wait. That's how it used to be. No one can wait for anything anymore.

I cruise into Little Rock, taking I-30 southbound, crossing over the Arkansas River and exiting off into downtown. I putter along President Clinton Ave. and spot the Peabody and turn in, park and go inside. A guy with spiked blonde hair and a black suit says hello. I tell him I need a room for one night. He types and says a few things about this and that. I nod, yes, yes, yes, that's fine, through all of it until he asks for a credit card and then asks me to sign. I go back out to my car and drive off, going nowhere really, turning down roads, stopping, yielding in and around downtown. I drive south on Main, going over I-630, when I spot Juanita's on the right and remember how hungry I am. I park on the street in front and tell the young lady I'd prefer a booth if she has one.

I get the booth and the cheese dip and guacamole as an appetizer. The booth is back in the corner beyond the doorless entry to the kitchen. I can faintly hear playful Spanish spoken in the kitchen. I think about whether the guys in the back have families or not across the border. I sit with my back to the wall and dip the chips into the little bowls. The waitress asks how everything is and I tell her fine and that I want a Juanita's chicken burrito. I've been here before, ten years or so ago with the Fergusons. They said it was the best Mexican place in all of Arkansas. I told them they were right as we left. Here I am again, ten years later. I'm glad it's still here and that I drove by because it's exactly what I need right now.

Ten years ago I was not married. I was twenty-nine, not thirty-nine. I spent a lot of my time outside. Whether I was at Momma's house or my own, I would often ask to take conversations outside or just plant myself in some of the furniture on the porch. I slept outside a lot, too. Sometimes I'd go sit in the grass, lay in it and nap, the sun's warmth coating me with a cheery drowsiness. That's how I spent most of my twenties, laying around, whether it was outside or inside.

I was eager to get my own home after I dropped out of Arkansas State for good. I would wander around Momma's house, muttering to myself. Birdshit would look up from the living room couch once in a while, her fingers still moving across those invisible keys, giving me a questioning look. Lou had come down to take care of the paperwork. He said, "You sure this is the house you want?" I said yes, and he pointed to where I was to sign my name in cursive and he said don't worry about the rest. A few days later the house was mine. He handed me the keys and got in his king-size pickup truck and drove back up to Kansas City. I've been in that house ever since.

I remember the first night I was in it by myself after my new furniture was delivered and the movers had hauled over a small truck of stuff from Momma's. I stood out back on the small deck and scanned the reaches of my property with my eyes. After doing this for an hour I went inside, laid down on my couch which sat under the big windows in the living room, kicked my shoes off and sat there staring up into the sky watching yellow daylight turn to a dark blue or purple and then finally black. I didn't have a vision like Birdshit's recurring episode of her own murder or one of the brightly colored visions my daddy would describe to me in detail, it was subtler, less definite. It seemed that my mind was slipping away, if I would just let go. Almost like it wanted to go away, somewhere lonely, all by itself. It did not scare me. I wanted to go away too. I thought a lot about that and other things for the next nine years.

The food is as delicious as I remember. I ask for another basket of chips to scrape the sides of my salsa, guacamole and cheese bowls. I ask for a refill on my soda and lean back, push my plate across the table. More people fill the tables around me. There are several parties of six or more. The noise is louder, the aroma of grill smoke and beer breath fills the restaurant. Outside it is getting dark and I watch, focusing on a spot and watch it change colors until it is black.

After I pay, I wander down Main Street a short ways. Kids are lined up outside for a show in the adjoining stage room at Juanita's. They're dressed in mostly black with black hair hanging over their faces. They watch me with curiosity as I pass. I'm wearing white tennis shoes, faded blue jeans and a generic blue polo shirt. I look like a tourist.

I stop and ask one of the kids what band they're waiting to see. They tell me, a band called Doggie Door. "What kind of music does Doggie Door play?" I ask.

"Pretty much hardcore stuff. It's kind of punk, kind of metal. They're fucking awesome!"

"Sounds like it," I say, stuffing my hands into my jeans and waddling off slowly.

Beyond that is a pool hall. A few people mill about outside, smoking cigarettes, intently watching the cars that drive by. They look at me and then forget me. For a second I think about going in and getting in on a game but then decide against it. I can shoot pool pretty well but I can't shoot the shit all that great. And in places like this the shit you talk is more important than anything. I turn around, passing the kids again. The same kid who told me the name of band steps in front of me. "I got an extra ticket if you want."

"That's all right. I appreciate it though."

"You sure? They're letting us in right now. No one is going to buy this from me."

I turn and see that the line is beginning to move. Several kids jump up and down with excitement.

I take the ticket and get in line.

When Doggie Door comes to the stage and begins playing, the kids go apeshit. I'm surprised to discover people my age inside although they're not dressed like me. They're in full costume, the black everything theme which is so prevalent. I look like an after-school special father looking for his 13 year-old daughter who has run away from home. The singer seems to spit more than he sings and uses every profanity he can muster in between songs. "Everything sucks" is the theme: parents, life, work, job, the government. I can certainly understand such nihilism. I can rightly or wrongly understand why people feel this way. I feel this way too. I just don't punch my friends in the face and dance around in a circle to express it. Maybe they know something I don't. It doesn't take long for the kids around me to notice that I'm staring. An old man staring at young girls. It's biological, it's nature, I can't help it, and we all do it. But I'm creeping people out and I seem to make the youngsters nervous. So I leave.

Chapter Twenty

I WOKE UP IN MY CAR. I don't know when or why I parked in the Harvest Food's parking lot. My back is stiff. There are more missed calls on my phone. I start the car and drive down the street to the River Market. I find a parking spot in front of a pizza and beer place. It's too early for pizza and beer. I wander to the downtown library and pick up random books off the New Arrival shelves. The first thing I always do is check out the author photograph. I like clean shaven, youthful looking authors, man or woman. I shy away from the beard and glasses writer look or beard and bald or abundant disheveled hair and three days' beard look. A homeless man sits on one of the benches in front of the shelves, his legs crossed in a feminine or refined manner, carefully turning each page as he reads. He's wearing a San Francisco 49ers sweatshirt that used to be white. He has a mangy beard and thick gray hair.

"What are you reading?"

He looks up, "Poetry. It's a book of James Dickey poetry."

"No kidding. He's from Arkansas, right?"

"No. South Carolina. You're probably thinking of Miller Williams."

I don't know who he's talking about but agree, "Yeah, that's right. My sister writes poetry. She's published a book. And actually has a new one coming out later in the year. Her name is Bridget Shiloh. But we call her Birdshit."

He laughs and snorts and a little bit of snot hangs from his nose. "Why do you call her that?"

"It's one of those things."

"Right. It's like when my ex-wives, all three of them, asked me why I drink so much. I'd say that too. It's one of those things." He snorts again. I notice that there's now more snot, some of it dangling from the tip of his nose.

"Maybe you should quit drinking. Or at least try to."

"I've tried to. The A.A. people told me to turn over my control and drinking problem to a higher power. I did that. And I still drank. So I came to the conclusion that my higher power was a colossal dick. Either that or there's no such thing." He looks around cautiously realizing he is talking loudly. "Besides, poets drink. They're here. And so am I. We keep each other company."

"I'd say you're about right on those conclusions of yours."

The homeless man abruptly stands up and leaves, without explanation or a farewell gesture. I stroll through the rest of the first floor, debate about going upstairs, decide against it and leave.

I stand outside the library and watch construction workers tear down the wall on a building across the street. I see what appears to be a mental hospital looming to my left, imperious and impassive. I see a yellow trolley car float past to my right. I amble back the way I came, then cross another street and ask a passing police officer where I can get on the trolley. He points behind him and I see a small group standing on a corner. There is an encased brochure explaining the different routes for the different cars. I decide I want to take the one that goes over the Broadway Bridge into North Little Rock and comes back again. Bridges bother some people. They feel unsafe—what if I fall in, they'll say. I wish we didn't have bridges. Though not for that reason. I wish we had to go *underwater*.

The group is comprised of tourists. Their accents sound Midwestern although I'm not an expert in these things. I look the other way when they attempt eye contact, fearing they may be from Overland Park and will molest me with their self-importance. I once listened to some poor guy who talked about his job for twenty minutes. If you spend twenty damn minutes of your free time, of your life, telling some stranger about your job then you probably belong in places like Overland Park. He was a "product developer" of some type. They developed products to sell. I thought if I had a valid concealed gun permit I would've then and there pulled it out from hiding and shot him in the mouth so he'd quit talking. Finally, it came out in a flurry. I said, "Will you shut the hell up?" Sometimes it slips.

The trolley approaches and we board in single file fashion.

After we've all loaded on and dropped our dollar bills into the pay-slot our conductor yells, "Howdy folks!"

"Howdy folks" is not what I wanted to hear. I want to enjoy a peaceful, introspective, contemplative trolley ride.

The guy reminds me of our tour guide in Hannibal, Missouri. Bree, Sparkman and I went up there two summers ago. She didn't want to go. She had no idea who Mark Twain was and didn't care. I told her not to worry; most of the people who visited Hannibal didn't know who Mark Twain was either. But everyone knows who Tom Sawyer is right? Huck Finn? I told her to stay clear of the strollers and fat-gutted fathers smoking Winston full-flavors and constantly readjusting their Budweiser ball caps. The only way I got them to go was to agree to a full day at Six Flags in St. Louis on the way back. They say marriage is about compromise, I say it's about appeasing warring parties.

The trolley goes down a street and veers back by the library over a few more blocks and then turns in front of the Peabody and the Old State House. The conductor tells us that Henry Miller once declared the Old State House to be the most beautiful building in the South. Someone asks who that is and apparently he's a writer of some notoriety. He liked to paint with watercolors as well, the conductor tells us.

We turn left, going up the incline of the Broadway Bridge. The engines get louder, they scream like they're in pain and roar once we level out. Halfway across he stops the trolley and recommends that people get out their cameras and snap away. Behind us is downtown Little Rock and all underneath us is the Arkansas River. I enjoy watching the water more than gazing at the buildings. The conductor gets it going again, down the bridge into North Little Rock. We meander through North Little Rock a bit, turn around, go over the bridge again and then we're back where we started. Everything looks exactly the same as when I left.

I get off and go find my car. Then I see that the beer and pizza joint is open and get a booth, order a small pizza with tomatoes and mushrooms and watch the 24-hour news assholes on the television screens hanging in the corner.

Chapter Twenty One

IT'S FIFTY MINUTES on the dot to Frothmouth from Little Rock. Forty minutes going east on I-40 and another ten minutes crawling along Highway 7A until you officially cross over into the town of Frothmouth, Arkansas. I pull my Honda into Garner's Gas & Snack. The Garner family has run it for the past 50 years. I fill up and go inside to pay. Coming out as I approach the door is Mayor Ferguson. He reaches his arms out and before I have time to react, he hugs me. "How you been," he says, letting go.

"Good, real good, you?"

"Good here too. My oldest is heading to law school soon."

"Where at?"

"The University of Chicago."

"That's great news."

"And you know all about Michael."

"I don't think so."

"Sure you do. Its okay, Odom. I'm fine with it. Y'all good people."

"What do you mean?"

"I know all about him up in Kansas City with your sister. Now, it's probably not the best thing for either of them or for the community—knocks Frothmouth down to 325 residents, now—but all things considered, you know, it's okay by me. Michael's always wanted to go off and do his thing. Get himself out of this small town. I understand that. I used to be a young man too. Right?"

I nod.

"Well, I said he can stay up there and work this summer. I talked to your Uncle Lou and he's keeping his eyes on things for me up there. Just between me and him, of course. Michael thinks he's his own man, right. So I'm letting him grow up. He's eighteen years old. But I told him he's coming back in August and he's going to school. He got accepted at UAPB but I'm kinda pushing him towards Philander-Smith."

He's waiting for me to continue. Share a piece of gossip. Mention the weather. Complain about gas prices or something.

"All right," he finally says. "Well, you drop in and say hi sometime. Been awhile since you been over for a Sunday night meal. You used to never miss 'em."

"I'll get over. I promise."

"Good. Well, I'll be on my way." He gets in his pickup truck and backs it out.

I say hello to the elder Mr. Garner when I go in. He's sitting in his chair watching the 13 inch television he has tucked under the counter. It's funny. Given the way they say things are headed, I would've thought that some Kuwaiti would have taken over this place, too. Or maybe they'll never be able to find it.

"Say there Odom, where you been?" he says, not taking his eyes off the screen. "A few folks say they hadn't seen ya in awhile. Say your Momma says you went on up north somewhere."

"Yeah, that's right." I take a 16-ounce orange soda from the cooler case. "I was up in Kansas City. Drove in from Little Rock just now." I set the soda on the counter.

"That's right. You was out on a little trip."

"Yessir. Had to go find my sister. She'd run off."

"I didn't know she needed to be found. I thought everyone knew she was going on up there and stay with that uncle of yours or something."

"No, she ran away."

Mr. Garner studies the television screen for a few seconds. "Well. Did you find her?"

"Yessir."

"She all right. Did you bring her back down?"

"No. She's still up there."

"That right? What's she doing?" Mr. Garner looks up at me for the first time.

"I don't know. I think she's going to stay up there for a while. I don't know. I didn't really ask. How much with the gas on pump two?"

He punches a blue button on his control panel that tracks the four pumps. He reads the red numbers, adds it to the cost of my soda. I give him the money and leave.

I pull my car around to the side and scroll through the missed calls on my phone. I have calls from Blakey, Lou, Bree, Momma and a few numbers I don't recognize. I call Bree at the house. No one answers. I call Momma but she doesn't answer either. Blakey picks up on the second ring and wants to know where I am. I rehash the last twenty-four hours to him. He sounds calm. He says, "Glad to know you're all right. What you doin' down there?"

"I don't know yet."

"Going to talk to Bree and your Momma?"

"Probably."

"You should do that."

"So how are you?"

"Good. Good. Good. Me and Trisha, well, we're getting along real fine. And that Luke boy and I have been running around a little. He's a good kid. He reminds me a lot of myself when I was his age. Smart but reckless. Lou's got me helping out some at the restaurant washing dishes with the Mexicans and learning some Spanish. Says if I do all bueno and whatnot, he may have something better lined up for me."

"Where are you staying?"

"Mostly at Trisha's."

"And Birdshit. What is she doing?"

"She's fine. She's hanging around the restaurant too. Lou's got her waiting tables a few hours here and there. It's been a little rocky; takes her awhile to warm up to new things. You know how she is. But the customers love looking at her, especially the lunch crowd, the construction workers and them boys. They tip her well. Michael is working there too, back in the kitchen mostly. Waits tables sometimes. Birdshit says she's thinking about playing the piano again and did she tell you she has a new book coming out?"

"Yes, a book of poetry."

"That's what I said a new book."

"Well, a book of poetry isn't exactly a book, Blakey. I mean a book of poetry is fifty pages long."

"Right." I hear Blakey talking to someone, his voice is low. Then he says, "Gotta run. You give me a holler if you need anything. And I mean anything."

"Hey! Whatever happened to Mateo Panadero? What was the story?"

"Oh, that, yeah, well, I got Luke on that and it's all taken care of."

"What? Taken care of. What does that mean?"

"Well, he used to work for me and I can tell you that he won't be employed as a private investigator in the State of Louisiana anymore."

"What happened? Why was he after Birdshit?"

"I don't know, Odom. Just make it whatever you want to believe."

"What's that supposed to mean?"

"Okay, well… it's like this then. Once Luke and I confirmed where Mateo was and what his motive was, Lou told us to step aside and made a phone call. We haven't seen Mateo around since. That's all I know, and quite frankly, all I want to know."

"That makes sense."

"Does it?"

I hesitated. "You tell me, Blakey. Is there more to it? Something you're not telling me?"

"Oh, no. That's everything. I was just wondering why it made sense, that's all. Never mind."

"Because I trust you, Blakey. I have to trust you."

"Why's that, Odom?"

"I don't trust anybody else. I don't even trust myself."

We lose our connection.

Highway 7A is the main road that cuts through all of Frothmouth. Most people live off of it or near it. My house is at the end of the road as they say. The end is where 7A joins with Highway 31. Highway 31 juts out west and if you turn right to go east, you won't get very far because it ends about a hundred yards down where it turns from gravel to dirt to grass. Just beyond that are the woods. They begin somewhere off in the distance and run on up through the northwest part of Frothmouth. This northwest part is where my Momma's house is. I'm three miles away. Where my property starts, the woods have ended. My land is flat, seemingly never-ending. But if you look off to your left the woods are still there, looking right back at you.

I follow 7A and drive to my house. It hasn't burned down, thankfully. Bree's minivan is parked inside the garage, the door open. I park on a patch of dirt that serves as guest parking when we have visitors. Inside I hear the ruckus of cabinets slamming shut, aluminum cans clanking. I walk into the kitchen. "Bree?" I shout.

She's putting away several bags of groceries; she turns around. "There you are. Been gone so long I had to go to the store. Sparky and I were about to starve."

"I've been telling you for years that the grocery don't bite. I don't have to do all the shopping."

"Yeah, well."

She does not seem surprised or all that interested in my arrival.

"How you been?" I say, picking up cans and reading the labels, shaking my head. The few times she has gone to the grocery on her own she always buys the expensive brands. She doesn't know how to shop. Why pay fifty cents more than we should for a can of green beans. For a short time she was on a vitamin kick and was swallowing twenty-some thousand milligrams of Vitamin C every day. She always bought the brands that were twice as expensive. I explained to her that all of these companies buy the exact same ascorbic acid from the exact same chemical suppliers. There's no difference. I would show her the active ingredients and how they were the same, bottle to bottle. She didn't believe me. She said that if there's no difference then why is one bottle only $2.99 and another bottle $5.99. That sounds like a difference of a hell of a lot to me.

I don't know how she's survived this long sometimes. Then I remember: she's beautiful. And she's had me to take care of her.

Later on after Sparky is asleep, we sit down to talk. It's taking her longer than I expected to get going. She's waiting on the tears to arrive before she can start the show. That's how she's always done it. The tears are a barrier that she uses, a lubricant, a tool. The tears are not coming. I can tell this performance will be a nightmare. This is what the end will be like.

Through dry eyes and a downturned mouth, she tells me that, "I think it's probably over." And then asks me if I agree. "I don't know," I say. Every statement is turned into a question, backing me into a corner until I give in, sit down and give up. She says, "This can't be fixed, right?" "Do you really think we can work this out?" "There's nothing left for us, right?" "You don't love me, do you?"

I've heard it before. Behind the magic curtain another man awaits, giggling, snickering in the darkness, listening to the spectacle. Maybe he's sitting outside, under the big window in the living room, capturing every word. Maybe I should go get my shotgun and kill her, kill Sparky, shoot this other guy in the balls and let him bleed to death, drive to Memphis and turn myself in for the murder of four people. Or shoot myself too.

Her rambling talk and maneuvering out of this relationship into the next one goes on for another hour. As much as I despise her, I am not ready for her to walk out the door. I care deeply about her in a way that she does not realize; in many ways I'm very much like her and she is like me. We've both died the same deaths already. We're both ghosts sauntering this world like the battlefield dead, lingering and not able to let go of the moment when our lives left us.

I feign some hope still. This frustrates her. Her job is to dispel all hope. She won't go until she receives my acceptance orders, until I unofficially say, "Okay." But I hold back. She stands up, paces and sits back down. She begins to plead with me and I tune her out remembering something my daddy used to say: People don't change, they just get better or worse.

After another hour Bree says, "Can I go? Is this over?"

"Okay."

"What's that?"

"Okay."

"That's it? We're finished?"

"Okay."

She stands up like she's really going to leave when I remember something. "You taking your son with you?"

"Can I leave him here for now?"

"Okay."

"Can you wake him up and make sure he gets to work on his school lessons? He knows what he's supposed to be doing. And then I'll pick him up in the afternoon sometime and explain what's going on. It'll be hard on him."

"I doubt that."

"And then this weekend we'll bring a truck over and get most of our stuff."

"Who are we?"

"Odom. Please."

She straps her purse on, evens out the waistline on her jeans and leaves. I go into the bathroom, jiggle the handle. It flushes. This is a good sign.

The next morning Sparky sleeps until 10:30. He comes into the living room, his hair standing up in every direction. I'm laying on the couch, looking out the window. Sparky says, "Is today Saturday?"

"No, it's a school day, Spark, speaking of which, how's that going? What are you learning about?"

"Science stuff. About space, the planets and stuff. Mom says the moon landing never happened. She said they filmed it in California."

"Why don't you go back to sleep."

"Where's Mom?"

"She'll be back."

"Okay. I'm going back to sleep."

It's mid-afternoon, sometime after three when Bree comes flying through the front door. Her eyes are thick with chemicals, probably been smoking weed and drinking some too. I look out the window and don't recognize the rusty red pickup or the guy driving it. I lay back down. She stomps straight into Spark's room. Then comes back to the living room.

"Why is he still in bed?"

"I don't know. Ask him."

"I told you to make sure he got up and did his schoolwork."

"And I didn't do it."

"Sparkman is already behind enough as it is with his school. He has to do his reading and writing lessons. He's only reading on a third grade level."

"Like I give a shit."

"I know you don't, Odom. You never gave a shit about anything other than your pathetic little life and your depressed old Momma and that fucked-in-the-head sister of yours."

I look at Bree. She sure has a low opinion of someone who played in the Little

Rock Symphony, can count backwards in any increment and is ambidextrous and got the same pretty-card balance from God to boot. I get up off the couch and walk up to Bree. She steps back. I smile at her. "This is my house you little cunt. And you can leave. Go get that retarded kid of yours out of here and don't come back. You tell your Marlboro man out there he can come by Saturday morning and I'll help him load up your crap into his truck. But I do not want to see you or Sparkman here, you understand?"

"Whatever."

"I'm not finished. And you will get court papers in the mail ASAP. This thing will be over just as quickly as the pickup truck fucks you've been getting all your life. I think that's fair. I think it's about time for you to leave."

"Fine, then," she says. "I don't ever want to see you neither."

"And the beauty is you won't have to."

"Well, I need to get some of my things then."

"Fine. You got twenty minutes to load up what you can. And like I said, you send over whatever his name is and we'll do the rest." I walk to the window and look out at the truck again. I try to make the face out. It's a Frothmouth face. "Is that Garner's oldest son in that truck?"

"Yep." Bree walks through the house picking up dirty clothes and stuffing them into trash bags.

"Gosh, how old is David nowadays? Fifty-five? Damn, Bree, he might be dead before this divorce is final. Might want to get yourself a backup plan set and going right quick. Ol' David out there, with him smoking his usual four packs a day, drinking beer for breakfast and whiskey for lunch and dinner, there's no telling how many more days that boy has left on his calendar. Hey, he ever think about coaching again? Or, has he not appealed the school board's decision to ban him from all school events?"

"Odom. You can shut the fuck up. Okay?"

"Yeah, you're right. I'm done. I mean, y'all make a cute couple. Well, I haven't really seen you two standing next to one another but I'd imagine that's a shot for a picture frame if you ask me."

Bree tells Sparkman to go sit in the car with David. The little hibernating shit says, "Who's David?" I can't help but to laugh even though it feels like one of those laughs where you do it to keep yourself from crying.

"Just get on out there in the truck. Here take this." Sparkman carries a bag full of clothes. Bree goes into our bathroom and starts throwing her cosmetics, lotions, razors and expensive fragrance collection into a suitcase. I follow her in there. "I'm going to have to find me a new place to buy gas and newspapers. That ol' boy David will be putting you to work up there at their store. You can count on that. The last time he had paid work was when Momma paid him a fifth of Old Crow to knock down Daddy's house and fill in the hole in our yard."

"He says I don't have to work." She brushes past me, knocking her elbow into my ribs.

"You could hit me harder than that if you really wanted to. But you don't because I protect you, Bree. You know that. I'm your fucking protector. I'm all you got."

"Don't tempt me, I could hit you if I wanted," she says, turning around.

"Come on back here and hit me if you really mean that."

"Why should I? All you'll do is hit me back."

"Hey now, you and I both know that's a lie. I never have and never would. You can be damned sure that drunk cripple you got out there in that truck will be laying down the law his way. I'm just trying to show you that you think you hate me and you created this mess in your head but it ain't even true."

"It is true, Odom. Why would I lie to my own damn self?"

"You been doing it your whole life Bree! You don't want to be with me, fine. But don't go running off with him, with *that*! And you know better. Goddamn you know better. Jesus Christ! Why? Huh? Don't do this to yourself anymore. It makes me sick."

She closes the suitcase, zips up an oversized duffel bag, carries them with her to the front door.

"I'll send David over Saturday morning and I'll have him write down his address so you'll know where to send me them divorce papers."

"Shit, Bree. I know where David lives. 150 Highway 7A. Frothmouth, Arkansas."

"That's where I live now too."

Chapter Twenty Two

THE NEXT MORNING I drive up to Frothmouth High School and wait to talk with Dr. Witten, the principal. He's pleased to see me when he finally comes out of his office and waves me back. I remain standing after he sits down. I tell him I want to make this quick and that there's nothing he can say or do to talk me out of it. "What's that?" he says.

"I'm resigning my position as the Assistant to the Assistant Football Coach and I will no longer be able to substitute teach or be a study hall monitor. Now, I'm not saying this is permanent just yet, but this will be how it is for a while now. I will let you know about next school year when I figure some things out and see how some pieces fall into place."

"Okay."

"So we're understood."

"Of course, Odom. Do what you need to do. Anytime you want to come back, you are welcome. Everybody here at F.H.S. has a lot of respect for you and we appreciate the work you do with the football team and filling in for those three weeks last year for Mr. Hester's Biology class when he was all busted up in the hospital after his car wreck."

"Yeah, can't say I taught them kids much about the nervous system but I know I learned a lot reading his notes and studying that textbook."

"We know you do a good job and that's why you are welcome back anytime. We care very deeply about you, Odom. This entire community supports you like we always have. And we always will. My door is always open. If there's ever anything you need to talk about or if you think you're not doing well… well, you know all that."

I extend my hand and approach the desk. He comes around from behind and takes my hand and we stand there shaking, trying to think of the next thing to say. We let go and I leave. I tell Mr. Witten's secretary, Barbara, that I like her new hairstyle.

I pull up to Garner's Gas & Snack. I leave the Honda running, walk inside with two quarters in my hand. I set the change on the counter, tell the senior Garner that's for the *Arkansas Democrat-Gazette*. "I know what it's for, Odom," he says, playing with the rabbit ears on his 13 inch television. "You come in here seven days a week and buy a paper. Never could figure out why you just didn't subscribe to the damn thing. Helluva lot cheaper, not to mention it's delivered to your house every day."

"I enjoy coming up here to buy it. I like the drive. Something to do, I suppose."

"Well, all right, go get yourself a copy and I'll be seeing you tomorrow like always."

"Say Mr. Garner, how's your oldest boy? David? How's he doing nowadays?"

"He's doing about what he's always done. Not much. You know he works one or two nights for me here, closing up on Friday and Saturday nights mostly."

"Oh yeah? I don't get around here come nighttime. So that's probably why I never see him."

"That and you don't drink do you Odom?"

"Not really."

"Well, if you were a drinker you'd be seeing a lot more of David."

"I've heard. Whatever happened with him and that brown-haired lady from Camden? He was bout set to marry her last I knew."

"They did get married. Then they got a divorce."

"No kidding. Why'd they divorce?"

Mr. Garner folds his arms in front of his body and leans back into his chair. "Ah, David gets to drinking, and then he likes to fight, even if it's his own wife. She put him in jail long enough to get out of town."

"That right?" I stare off to the left of Mr. Garner, looking at the stacks of warm six-packs of Miller Lite sitting on the floor.

"Yep. Think David's too old to learn new tricks."

"Yeah," I say, still staring at the beer, "he's an old dog all right."

"Thought you'd already heard about that, Odom."

"I haven't been as up on Frothmouth happenings this past year or so."

"You're right about that. People say they don't see you around much anymore, except for when they drive by and see you out there on your porch sitting by yourself."

"Yessir. I imagine that's where you'd find me."

"Well, you go on and get. No point in wasting your time talking to a man as old as I am. I got me that Old-timer disease. Ever heard of it?" He coughs out a short, hard laugh.

"That's a good one Mr. Garner. You ain't really old, you just look it, that's all."

"Get on outta here, Odom." He waves me off and goes back to his television.

I almost leave without picking up a newspaper.

There's not much going on in the paper. People fighting and making distinctions between themselves and other people who look and act just like them so that they have a reason to fight. I read the sports in great detail, noting the Mid-South bowling champs and studying the recruiting reports for the football Razorbacks. But mostly I enjoy reading the editorials. They're pure comedy. There's the hard-right-leaning columnist who expounds on the ethics of responsibility and economic virtue and then secretly files for bankruptcy. The left-leaning columnist is one of those Ozark hills hippies who's been riding a bike for thirty years and thinks bathing is a weekly chore. She's pissed because the world isn't nice enough for her. There comes a time in most people's lives when they realize that the world is not a nice place, not a fair place at all and you nudge yourself into the fight and hold your ground the best you can. The ones who can't hold on, they move to the hills or lay low or become criminals, both the legal and illegal kind. The legal kind who sit at a desk and wear suits and get three years probation for stealing two millions dollars, and the illegal kind who work out of their one-bedroom apartment, wear Atlanta Hawks jerseys that hang to their knees, steal a five-hundred-dollar stereo and go to prison for eight years.

I'm so sick of it I crumple the thing up before I'm even through with it.

I try calling Birdshit but there is no answer.

I sit on my porch for a while.

There's nothing left to look at.

I walk inside and find my daddy's old shotgun in the bedroom closet, wipe it down, load it and put it in the trunk of my Honda.

I get in and drive around a bit. I drive to Garner's Gas & Snack and turn around. I do this sixteen or seventeen times. Each time it's still just the senior Garner's beat-up Ford Taurus parked on the side of the building. No one pumping gas, no one buying snacks. It's mid-morning. Most Frothmouth folks are at work. A few sit at the only bar in town; it opens at ten each morning. You wouldn't know it was a bar if it didn't have a Budweiser sign hanging out front next to the door. Otherwise you'd think it was a red brick building abandoned by some failed industrialist. People kind of pretend the place doesn't exist. Even the cops stay away from it. They figure drunken fights aren't worth their time. Fights are bound to happen and just putting people in jail for fighting never seemed like much sense if people were going to fight anyhow. Might as well let them fight it out and just drive by on patrol and look the other way.

There are three cars and two trucks parked along the front. I pull in and turn off the Honda next to the only vehicle I recognize. A rusty red pickup truck.

When I open the door, everyone inside looks up at the same time as if it were choreographed. I quickly shut the door behind me, sealing off the sun. They all turn back to their drinks except for one. There's a low hum of music in the background although there's no telling who or what is singing if anyone is even singing at all.

The bartender is Rodney Carson's boy. Rodney Carson played for the football Hogs back in the early 1960s and played three seasons professional football with

Cleveland. Then he came back to Frothmouth, opened a bar, had a family and died. Now his son, who is my age, runs the place. Everyone calls him Little Rodney because he looks just like his daddy although his name is Paul. He played football for Frothmouth and one forty-yard punt return for a touchdown was the farthest distance he ever managed to get from this town.

I take a seat at the end of the bar in front of Little Rodney. He stands there waiting for me to say something. "A Budweiser."

Little Rodney reaches into the cooler case and pulls out the bottle. He twists the top off and makes a show of jump-shooting it into the garbage can at the other end of the bar. I give him a five-dollar bill, he gives me back three and I push one dollar back at him and he picks it up and puts it in his front right pocket.

I take a sip. It tastes like beer. I figure I'll be lucky to drink half of it.

I look straight ahead, reading the labels on all the bottles. Out of the corner of my eye I see someone lean over and look down at me, his eyes fixed, not going anywhere. It's a stalemate. No one is moving or saying anything.

"Well, hell. Odom Shiloh in here this time of day," David Garner says. "Didn't know we were privileged folks today with our special guest."

One of the patrons coughs into his fist and says that he doesn't ever recall seeing me in here before. Another one concurs with this thought. "Nope, never have," he says.

"Howdy to you too David." I force another drink, set the bottle back down, spinning it around and around in my hand.

He's still leaning and looking with an intensity I hadn't seen in awhile. "If you're hoping to find Bree, you ain't gonna find her here and she ain't coming up this way. She's back cleaning up my place, scrubbing it down real good like a real woman. Odom here did all the lady work hisself at his place." He waits for some kind of reaction from this announcement. No one is stirred by his comment. Someone orders another beer. A cigarette is lit and I'm amazed how much smoke can come from one little cigarette. I watch the trajectory of the smoke as it is delicately carried away and spirals upward.

"You treating her right David?" I continue to stare ahead.

"Yessir. Better and better everyday. She's learning real good. Learning things someone forgot to teach her."

"That right?" I read the label on a Jameson whiskey bottle over and over. Jameson Jameson Jameson. My eyes don't move. "Hell, David. You can barely write your own name and still piss yourself at night, what can you teach a grown woman?"

He smacks his beer bottle down on the bar. I glance over at him. His anger comes at me like a gush of hot wind. Little Rodney walks up to David and leans in close and whispers. Someone else is patting him on the back. I get the feeling they've seen this before.

"Now boys, just 'cause he still pisses hisself don't mean he can't be a man and come outside and talk with me for moment. That all right with you, David?"

David is walking out the door before I have time stand up. I turn around before I leave and tell them I don't want to see that door open again until I come back in. "Y'all stay in here and drink your beer. I'm not gonna hurt him. We're just talking, grown man to grown man."

I close the door and find David holding his fists in the air about six inches apart bouncing in front of his face. "Is this why you came here Odom? Well, you got it."

"Put your fuckin' hands down David. Come over to my car, I got something of Bree's she forgot."

"I thought I was coming over Sunday to get the rest of her stuff."

"You are, on Saturday, not Sunday. I imagine the days of the week get away from you when you don't have a job. But this is some of her feminine stuff she might need. You know what I mean."

He drops his hands from the air into his pockets, kicks a rock along a path and shuffles to my car. I unlock the trunk and pull it open. I see Daddy's gun and somehow I omit sequenced increments of time because the next thing I'm aware of is having both hands on the gun and pointing it at David. I hoist it up shoulder -level like I'm about to fire. I am aiming the weapon and telling him to move it, to go around to the back of the building. There are no windows in the bar, the front door is closed. We will be alone. He is walking around to the back of building where no one can see us, turning around every few feet to protest; I am keeping my sight on him, my finger touching the trigger. I am walking one step at a time behind him.

"Get down on your knees." He drops to one, then the other.

"Jesus Christ, Odom. Put that gun away and we'll settle this the right way. Throw that gun down and get your fists up."

"You wanna die?"

"What do you mean?"

"Open your mouth."

"What are you talking about?"

"Open your mouth like you're getting ready to suck a dick." I put the barrel to his face, nudge it on his cheeks. "Open your mouth!"

"Fuck you!"

I land my right heel on his forehead. It surprises him and he falls back and I follow that with another kick, this time to his nose which crunches under my weight. I step back, aiming the gun again and wait. It's almost like he was knocked out for a few seconds because when he sits himself up, he gazes at me like he's just woken up from a nap. Then he sees the gun and me, and he realizes all of this is real.

"Open your mouth." He does and I jam the barrel all the way until I hit his throat, he gags and his eyes water.

I hold the barrel steady. "Are you scared motherfucker?"

He nods his head very slightly, the double barrel fitted into his mouth. His eyes are frozen on mine, red, watery, completely stuck. Blood drips from both nostrils.

I hit him again.

"Are you scared yet?"

He nods again, this time very slowly.

"Scary ain't it. How do you think Bree felt when you raped her? Had your sick little way with her? Huh? What kind of disgusting things did you make her do? Tell me."

He shakes his head. I take the gun out of his mouth. He catches his breath, "I didn't do nothing like that, Odom. Shit, man."

"It don't matter with sick fucks like you. Little girls. Little boys. Big boys. Big girls. Does it?"

He looks up, second guessing me. "What in the hell are you talking about?"

"Open your mouth again and suck that barrel like it's a big fat cock."

I shove the gun in his mouth. He doesn't move.

"You heard me. Suck it like the faggot you are."

He slowly begins to move his mouth up and down the barrel of the gun. "If you do a good job maybe I won't pull the trigger." I look around. We're still alone except for the wind and the light above us. Then he really gets into it and I tell him to unbuckle his pants and pull down his underwear. I don't look but I can tell that's he's naked. I tell him to jam his fingers up his ass while he's sucking the barrel. He starts to do it. He closes his eyes while everything is happening. I tell him to show me his fingers, I want to see. His middle finger and ring finger are streaked brown with shit. I tell him to keep at it.

Then I'm no longer standing there holding the gun. I'm twenty yards away watching it happen. Then I'm standing on top of the bar, watching. David is working the barrel in and out of his mouth in a deliberate and fluid manner, and working his fingers in and out his rectum, knowing he has no choice.

I stand there from far away and watch the life fade from his face. I want to pull the trigger. I know I will unless I stop myself. I taunt him a little and pull the barrel out of his mouth and smack his face.

"Want to suck it some more?"

He sits there, resting on his knees, his dust stained jeans wrapped around his ankles, his right hand covered in shit, panting and out of breath. There's dark dried blood around his mouth and all over his lips. Fresh blood continues to ooze out.

"I can't hear you." I poke him in the forehead with the gun.

"Yessir."

"Okay, Yessir, what?"

"I want to."

"Okay, I want to what?"

He has to look down to say it. "To suck it."

"Okay. Okay. That's what I thought." He opens his mouth halfway and before I slide it back in I tell him to put his fingers in his mouth. He brings the fingers from his clean hand up to his mouth.

"No, no, no, you dumbshit. The *other* hand. This is the kind of shit you had Bree do, isn't it? She told me all about you. All the things you liked for her to do."

"Odom, I swear to God I don't know what you're talking about," he says, so quietly I can barely hear him, almost a whisper, as if he were uttering a prayer, trying to save himself.

He very slowly raises his soiled hand up in the air and looks at it; a layer of dirt and dust covers it now, clear-white tears dropping. The entire hand is covered in dripping brown gunk. "That's the one," I say. "Now put it in your mouth and suck all the juice off of it. Clean it off with your mouth." I point the barrel between his eyes and bump him with it; he grimaces. There's a fresh bruise forming right where I have the gun pointed. I poke him again, harder this time.

His middle and ring finger go in first.

I can see my finger on the trigger and I watch closely, trying to decide when I'm going to squeeze it and start things all over for myself once again.

He's coughing, and retching.

I can see a hole and his organs behind it.

I can see David dying before my eyes.

After another minute or so he's got most of his hand clean.

He's dead now.

"Now open up real wide for me." I put the gun in his mouth. He starts to shake, his crying smears the brown and red stains around his mouth; little sewage rivers flowing down his chin, running all the way down his neck and his chest.

I pull the gun out of his mouth, tell him he's a lucky son of a bitch and then swing it as hard as I can across his face and he falls to the dirt with his eyes closed.

Chapter Twenty Three

WHEN I GET HOME I take a shower. I stand there until the hot water runs out and then dry off and brush my teeth, getting the beer taste out of my mouth. My hair smells like watermelons and my skin smells like flowers. I used Bree's bodywash gel on accident. I slip on clean underwear, jeans and a black t-shirt I've had for many years. The thing won't fall apart. It's faded but it's still in one piece.

I don't usually watch much TV but I turn it on and sit there listening to the sound. The jingles and narrations for commercials are nonsense. The characters on the shows are not like any people I've ever met. They act like human beings trying to be human beings. I stop at a televangelist show. It looks local, low-budget. The preacher bears a striking resemblance to the man who talked to Blakey and me in the parking lot in Little Rock. He sits at a poorly constructed set with his Bible in hand. "It's glorious, isn't it," he says, staring at something above him on the screen. He says, "Can't you feel the glory? That's the glorious spirit. That's Jesus' love. Now, you'll see a number appear on the bottom of your screen…"

The next channel is a game show.

Then there's Oprah, again. That guy I heard in the shower in Kansas City is back on. Or, it's a repeat. I can't tell. I don't remember this part. I can tell that he's trying to sell something. A book. Oprah says, "Let's go back to what we were talking about earlier. About repairing the damage. You said that you have to confront the damage, right?"

"That's correct, Oprah. And we're all damaged. It's a matter of finding that damage, confronting it and repairing it."

An audience member asks if damage is just a new word for pain or suffering and if repair is simply a different word for healing or recovery.

"That's a very good question and I'm glad you asked." I always hate it when they say that. He continues, "If you repair it, then it's fixed. You never have to revisit it. But healing and recovery is a process, it takes time, a long time. And frankly, who has time anymore?"

The audience hoots and hollers and Oprah looks into a camera, smiling, "Lord knows this girl don't have the time for healing. I wanna be fixed *now.*"

"Exactly," Andrew stammers. Runs a hand over his beard. "And… and pain implies that something still hurts. Damage implies that it hurt at one time and it doesn't necessarily hurt anymore but you still have to fix it."

"You mean, repair it?" Oprah says.

"You see how quickly you've caught on?"

Oprah says, "So we repair the damage. We don't heal from the pain. Or recover from the trauma."

"You got it."

"So how do we fix it?"

"There are lots of ways."

I don't bother taking the shotgun out of the Honda. No one is going to come looking for me. I wonder if David will even show up on Saturday morning. If he does, none of this will be mentioned. It's forgotten, stored away in a place not quite like memory; it will be kept like blood, pulsing through every part of his body.

I go from room to room trying to figure out what Bree will want. I think of calling her to ask and then decide maybe I should wait a few days. There's the computer she bought but rarely used. I wouldn't mind keeping it. I used it more than she did. It's nice to know that whenever something comes to my mind I can sit down, type it on the screen and an answer will appear.

Sparky's bedroom furniture will no doubt go bye-bye. I figure I'll get me a new bed, throw it in there and keep it as a guest room, like it was before Sparky took it over. Never had a guest but you never know. All the furniture in the master is mine. And in the third bedroom: the computer, storage cabinets and bookshelves. Bree may have a plate or two and a serving spoon that's hers in one of the drawers. Over the years I've collected an interesting assortment of plates and glasses from several ex-girlfriends and Mona. I've got lids that don't fit anything and pans of every size, color and degree of wear and tear. It's probably a good time as any to start collecting this crap and taking it down to the Franks County dump. That's just what I'll do.

In no time I've filled the entire front and back seat of my Honda with trash bags full of utensils, pots, pans, chipped glasses and stained serving bowls. I find four stacks of Bree's magazines and toss them on top of my pile in the back seat. The magazines explode, making a loud smacking sound on impact and flying all over the place.

In a final sweep of the house, I carry a box with me and toss in knick-knacks and decorative ornaments whose origins I've forgotten. Small wooden painted birds and glass sculptures shaped like bells and a miniature cowboy boot that has been holding the same three pens in it for twenty years. Who gave me this one? A theater major from Jonesboro. Before throwing it away, I click the end of one of the pens to see if it works and it does. I'm delighted. Twenty years later. Then I throw it in the box.

In the hall closet I pull down the old raggedy green blanket I've had since I was a kid. I haven't used it in ten years, at least. I stuff it into the box. I even pull open the refrigerator and scour the shelves for past-date jars of grape jelly and olives. A to-go box that's been on the bottom shelf for three weeks pops open when I pitch it in the box with the rest. Two dried, shriveled chicken strips and a wad of dehydrated mashed potatoes that look like sand. I close it.

The trash bags fall over and split open as I drive up the short bumpy hill to the dump. The pans and magazines slide back and forth. There's a pickup leaving as I come up to the top of the hill and I veer left to give it room to pass. He waves and I do the same. I don't recognize him. Probably some squirrel from the next county over dumping hard drives full of kiddie porn and meth lab supplies. It happens from time to time.

There are three large industrial trash bins. They are marked: paper, wood, glass.

Off to the side is a heap of trash bags full of god knows what. I place three of the busted trash bags on that pile and do my best sorting through my recyclables. In what seems like no time I'm done and my car is empty again and I drive down the same bumpy hill I came up. I go back out a different way than I came in. I pass by the Pie Lady's house. It's a heavily weeded house that's open one day a week. And the day of the week is never the same. The only way to know is to drive by and see if there are other cars out front. People drive over from Memphis, up from Monroe, Louisiana and even further to get one of her homemade pies: cherry, apple, blueberry, cinnamon, peanut butter, you never know what she'll make. And when she sells out, she sells out. Sometimes she sells all her pies before noon and you have to wait until the next week. Birdshit and I used to camp out there Friday nights when we were kids, in the hopes she'd be open the next day. I remember holding up a flashlight to her while she slept. Her fingers moved over their invisible piano, making shadow puppets on the grass.

I find the little road not too far off from the river. It's a quiet place at the end of a road that hasn't been used in a long time. I park under a cluster of trees.

From far off you can see the trees because there's nothing else around them for a good two hundred yards or so. But I like to park under the three biggest trees in the shade and roll down all of my windows. It's a hiding place in a way, because depending on how you're looking, it would be difficult to see me and my Honda here. Driving along you'd never know I was sitting here. It's like I don't even exist.

I lower my eyelids and drift slowly through the shadows behind my eyes. I find sleep but move past it, beyond sleep. I focus entirely on the wind polishing my face. I think about going back, back to sleep, but decide to stay out here for a while.

My phone rings and it wakes me up.

Momma's house is a drive I could make with my eyes closed. I've tried to do it before and come pretty close. Down the same road, three gentle bends in each direction. As I get close to it, I see the sole illumination coming from the front living room, where she sits facing the television day and night, checking off her shows like a to-do list. I kill the lights on the Honda, steer it around to the back and bring it to a stop about 200 yards from the house. I hit the trunk button, get out and quietly shut the door, extinguishing the car's interior lights. The light in the trunk is burned out and I have to feel for the gun I'd set underneath a blanket that came with the emergency roadside kit my insurance company gave me for signing up with them. I find the flashlight and gun, put the flashlight in my front pocket and hold the gun in front of me, across my body, aiming to the side and downward. I push down the trunk and when it shuts it makes a higher pitched sound than I remember.

I immediately begin a straight-line trek towards the woods. They spread out before me like the inside of a giant U, beckoning me further and further inside its reach. These are fields and grass and plants I've trampled over many times since I could remember. Sometimes I ventured out on my own; sometimes Daddy had to drag me out to the woods by my arm or my leg. Said that however hot and heavy things got, the Shilohs would always have the woods. Daddy taught me good.

I turn around and gauge the distance from Momma's house and know that I'm getting close. It was the house, not the woods that reassured my sense of place. It was always looking out from the woods onto the house that anchored me. At least until you go in deep enough. Then the arms of the trees spread around you and engulfed everything.

Right now the trees surround me on all sides except for directly behind me. The moon's hint is faint and the contrast between sky and treetops is two varying shades of black. I wonder if Blakey would call that romanticism. Somehow I doubt it.

I pull the flashlight out and flip it on and randomly point it at the trees, cut the beam back and forth. I walk on into the woods. I hear the crunching of leaves and the snap of twigs breaking; the tension of thick sticks bending under my feet. The ground is dry. It has not rained in weeks, maybe months. The air is warm but not hot. There is no glimmer of cold, only a feeling suspension.

"Daddy."

I keep walking until I no longer can see Momma's house when I turn around. Shoulder-high branches stab me; low-hanging limbs almost trip me.

"Daddy, are you there?"

My flashlight flickers. I stop to fiddle with it, turning it off, taking out the batteries, shaking them and putting them back in. The flashlight's beam no longer flickers.

"Daddy, can you hear me?"

I hear something. It's not necessarily a voice but a response. "Daddy?" I call out again.

I shine the light up and down and from time to time turn around. I slow down, taking a step every ten seconds or so. Then I hear it again, in sync with the sound of my voice. But it's not intelligible.

"Daddy, are you mad at me? I've come to see you again."

I turn off the flashlight and listen in the darkness. The slightest transfer of weight from one foot to another sets off a barrage of noises, leaves cracking, sticks snapping. My hands are sweaty, the shotgun slips from my grip but I catch it before it falls.

"Daddy, I've come to see you again."

You didn't tell your mother you're out here, did you Odom?

The gun is knocked out of my hands and falls to the ground setting off another reaction of fracturing noises. And the flashlight works itself loose from my pocket as I run back to Momma's house, waving my hands in front of my face, thrashing aside the branches and limbs.

Chapter Twenty Four

THE SCREEN DOOR is still swaying back and forth. Momma wants to know what in the hell has happened to me. I have trouble catching my breath. She sits me down on the faded red couch then pushes me over to the side and tells me to lie down. Momma gets a quilt from the guest room and spreads it over me. Then she gets the first aid kit from under the kitchen sink and looks over my hands and face. Eventually I calm down a little and tell her I was in the woods but that's all I can get out.

"And what? Did a wild hog come atcha and that's why you got yoself all tore up? We got dem hogs all over this place, Odom. You know betta than be sneakin' round them woods at night."

"Momma, there ain't no hog after me."

"You sit still and let Momma take a good look at you."

She turns on the lamp next to the couch and holds my face in her hands, examining me. She dabs some alcohol on a cotton ball and then taps it on my forehead, cheek and chin. It stings but I ignore the pain and don't bother making a sound. "Haven't seen my only boy in six months and he comes bangin' on my door at ten o'clock at night. Bangin' like a mad man, screamin' my name like a little boy, Momma let me in, Momma let me in, just like you used to, Odom."

"Yes, Momma."

She puts a band-aid on my forehead and says the other two wounds are just a nick and a little cut. Then she goes to work on my hands and forearms. They're full of scrapes and scratches like someone took the tip of a knife and sliced up and down and sideways all over the place. She cuts off a long strip of gauze and wraps it around my left forearm. The blood soaks through in one place about three inches long. I watch the gauze marinate in blood.

"Thank you, Momma."

"It's alright. You sit still, I ain't done yet. Whatcha doin' out in the woods?"

"I wasn't in the woods, Momma."

"I say you're lyin' or denyin' something."

"No Momma."

"Did your daddy tell you to lie to your momma's face 'bout where you been?"

"Yes Momma."

"Now Odom, you know that your daddy ain't out in them woods anymore."

"No Momma, I just saw him."

"You saw your daddy?"

"Yes. I mean, no, Momma. I heard him."

She looks up into my eyes, holding the gauze in her hand and after a second she drops her gaze and goes back to wrapping my arm. I twist my arm when the pressure makes it hurt and she tells me to be careful. She's thinking real hard about something as she treats my arm and I keep looking down at her waiting for her to say something. "Odom. Your daddy ain't in them woods any longer."

"He is. I was gonna go find him."

"And do what when you found him?"

"I was gonna shoot him. Shoot him dead. He's crazy. Everyone says so. I think I say so now. He sits out there all these years, Momma, sitting out there calling my name, wanting me to come back and bring him something. Bring him bottles, bring him food, bring him me. I can't do this anymore, Momma. He's got to get outta of my mind."

Momma drops the gauze and scissors and grabs me by the shoulders and shakes me. "Look at me, boy!" She smacks me cold across the face. I look right in her eyes. I've never had a problem looking at her. Momma was a real human being; I get something back from her. I never could look at Daddy's face. His eyes went on forever. They never stopped. "Are you looking?"

"Yes Momma."

"Are you listenin'?"

"Yes, Momma."

"Good. This is the last time I tell you this. Your daddy's gone. He's been gone a long time. He ain't never comin' back, Odom. He was a crazy man. Your daddy was crazier than a starvin' rabid dog, but he's gone. They took him. He left. He's been gone a long time, Odom. Why you forgettin' this, I don't know."

"Yes, Momma. Daddy's gone, Momma. I remember now. I remember now," nodding my head.

I lower myself to Momma's lap, resting the side of my face along her thigh. I take several deep breaths, repeating quietly to myself that he's gone, Daddy's gone. Momma presses her hands along the curvature of my skull, distributing the hairs on my head in a serene wave. "Everything's alright, Odom. Daddy's gone. Momma's here. Momma's here."

"Daddy's gone, Momma."

"That's right Odom."

We stay like this for a while. Our voices gradually quiet to silence, the only movement in the room is Momma's fingertips delicately layering the strands of my hair one on top of another. The only thing I feel right now are the tears that are taking their slow time dropping from Momma's face, landing on my neck. I count, like they say you're supposed to after you see lightning and see how long it takes for the next one to land.

"Momma," I whisper. "Why you crying?"

"I ain't cryin, I'm rememberin'."

The next day I wake up and it feels different, like the first day of your vacation when you open your eyes and realize you're not getting up for school. That you've got palm trees and a sand beach outside. You know it's supposed to be pleasant. But your rhythm is all thrown off. Today has to be the day I've been waiting for. I'm going to go underwater again.

I lie under the soft warmth of Momma's quilt and flip the pillow over to the other side and remain quiet. I hear Momma in the kitchen, opening cabinets, turning the water on and off. I smell bacon frying and feel the sun shining.

I cannot tell what time it is, but it is not early. The sunlight is too dull for early morning, too mature. I strain to look around the corner of the couch for the clock that hangs on the wall next to the kitchen entrance but I can't see it without completely adjusting my position. To adjust I'd have to sacrifice the stored-up warmth. I forget it.

On the floor next to the television is a stack of magazines, women's magazines. They must be Birdshit's. And right next to the magazines is a pile of books, thin books, not even a half inch thick. Probably poetry books. And a notebook on top of it, spiral bound and well worn. To the right of the couch is Momma's chair with her card table nearby where she keeps her remote, glasses, television guide and snacks. On the other side is what was Daddy's chair a long time ago. So long ago I can hardly remember him sitting in it. Nowadays it's the guest chair. What kind of guests, I'm not sure. I've never seen Birdshit sit in it. She's always on the couch, usually lying down with headphones on or with a book in her face or with a pillow tucked under her neck watching television. The last time I was over for a visit, I stood in the living room the entire time.

I peel the quilt off and sit up and throw my arms up in the air and stretch and make wake-up noises with my throat. Momma hollers from the kitchen. "You awake?"

"Yes, Momma."

"Hungry?"

"A little."

"Got eggs and bacon and coffee on in here."

"Thanks, Momma."

I get up and go to the bathroom, the one off the living room, a half bathroom with a toilet, sink and towel rack. I look at myself in the mirror. My face is covered in scratch marks. I go back into the living room and then walk down the hallway and open Birdshit's door. Her bedroom is the same as I remember. It's still decorated like a young teen's room except the Scott Baio posters are gone. But the pastel colors and girlie arrangement still reigns. Stuffed animals litter the floor; there are a few on a bean-bag and a dozen arranged on her twin bed. The bed frame is pink and the blanket is yellow and she has a red wooden desk that she's had since she was a little girl. The only difference is she's had to replace the original chair with a larger one. On it still sits an IBM Selectric typewriter. Frothmouth High School gave it to her for being the fastest typist. She typed 120 words a minute. It was insane how fast she typed and to think she uses that skill to type poems that are only nine or ten lines long. It must take her three seconds to write a poem. I remember how she'd get going on that typewriter and it'd sound like a herd of miniature horses galloping over a Western plain. There's a bookshelf on the floor under the window, between her desk and bed. It is full of books on the top self and stacks of spiral notebooks on the bottom.

I sit down at her desk and pull open the two drawers; it's full of loose papers and credit card bills, lots of credit card bills. The sums are enormous, and the colors of the numbers have changed from black to blue to red over time. There are pictures on the papers; she's drawn flowers and clowns and faces and trees, interwoven with the numbers. I dig through the drawers and find more pictures of woods and trees, some with smoke coming from the woods. One is a picture of a forest fire out of control.

There's a photograph of the two of us when we were kids and Momma is in the background. There are not many pictures of us when we were young. Daddy hated picture-taking and besides we didn't celebrate holidays. There was never anything to celebrate in our house. Christmas, Halloween, Thanksgiving all of those momentous occasions slipped by us year after year without mention. It was another of those Shiloh things. Sometimes after Daddy had quieted down in his shed, late at night, Momma would wake us up and drive around Frothmouth looking at the Christmas lights decorating the houses. One time we drove all the way to Little Rock in the middle of the night and drove through the rich neighborhoods on top of Cantrell hill. That night we'd stayed in a hotel and had breakfast in a diner. When Birdshit asked why we weren't going home Momma said, "Isn't it nice to have breakfast in a diner?"

I wish there was a picture of Daddy. I'd like to see him again. See if the way I remember him is what he really looked like.

Momma says my name and I turn around. She's standing in the doorway. "I don't know if Birdshit would much appreciate you bein' in here."

"I'm leaving Momma." I set her drawings and credit card bills back in her drawers.

"Well, once you get done eatin' you holler, there's something I need to talk to you about."

"What is it, Momma?"

"Now I just told you to go eat and then holler, now didn't I?"

"Yes, Momma."

"Alright then. I'll be back in just a bit. Gotta run out and mail a few things."

"Okay, Momma."

There's a place set for me in the kitchen. I pour myself a cup of coffee and look out the little window over the sink. Watch Momma pull away in the green pickup she's always driven. I shake out Louisiana hot sauce on my eggs and bacon and then sauce up the orange juice. Breakfast is over in five bites. I wish there were more and if she hadn't put the dishes in the sink to soak, I'd probably break open a few more eggs. But Momma's got her routine and I don't want to take the chance on making a mess.

I take my cup outside and walk the perimeter of the house. Out back I stop and look into the woods, remembering my gun and flashlight are still out there. I imagine whereabouts I think they are and tell myself I'll go retrieve them later. I watch the wind blow an empty paper cup from a fast food restaurant. It scurries across the grass, stops and then goes again. I think about just walking out there and picking it up but instead I watch and hope it blows away out of my sight so I won't be thinking about it anymore. Wonder how far that cup had to travel to get here.

Momma's pickup comes barreling down the dirt road. Momma always throttles that old thing as hard she can. She must've forgotten something. She wasn't gone long enough to make it to the Franks County post office unless all she did was drop them off at Garner's Gas & Snack. The senior Garner is good about taking mail to the post office. He's got a big box back behind the counter that people can ask to have mail put in. He goes to the post office every Monday and Thursday. It saves a lot of folks the time and the expense of a trip to the post office, which is twenty-three miles each way.

"Back already," I say, meeting Momma halfway.

"Just dropped the mail off at Garner's."

"I figured."

"He's lookin' old, ain't he?"

"A little bit."

"You lookin' old too, my boy."

"You think so?"

"I'm pretty sure 'bout it."

I follow Momma into the house and then head to kitchen where I refill my cup. She tells me to have a seat, get comfortable and walks into her bedroom. The coffee is very hot, the final cup from the pot that's been sitting on the burner for the last hour. When she comes back into the room she's carrying a large manila folder and one of those 11x17 envelopes you mail off your taxes or house deed in. She carries them between both her hands like its heavy. The envelope is faded and old and is full of pen scribbles and crossed out numbers and notes. It isn't sealed, just a flap folded over the side. Momma reaches in and pulls out the contents as she sits down in her chair. A picture, a small one, falls to the floor. It's black and white, a snapshot taken in the olden days. I reach down and get it before Momma can. I glance at it while handing it to her, "Who is this?" I say.

"That there is your daddy."

"Really?" I retract my arm and bring it up under my eyes. "How old was he?"

"There, he's nineteen. I think. Lemme see." It only takes a second and there's recognition, a moment in history defined in some way for her. "Yep. Nineteen."

"It's funny," I say, studying the photograph, feeling the fold that runs across the middle of it and touching the worn corners, imagining how many times this picture has been looked at, how many people have held it just like I am now. "Doesn't look much like the way I remember Daddy."

"Well, Odom, that's because that there is your *real* daddy."

"I know who it is. I'm just saying. You know how they say memory is tricky sometimes."

"That ain't memory. Like I said, that's your real daddy. There's no memory about it."

"What do you mean, my real daddy?"

"That's your daddy that helped birth you. He's your blood, Birdshit's too. The man you think of as your daddy was your step-daddy." She looks down and begins flipping through the paperwork.

I don't say anything.

Momma opens her mouth and then hesitates. She keeps her eyes focused on the paperwork, her fingers sorting, her mind thinking of her next move. I can feel it. She's telling herself that she just said it. It's out in the open. She said it. Shouldn't it be over now?

"Momma?"

"I just said it. I've been meaning to tell you for so long now but I just wasn't able."

"Momma. Who was Daddy? The man who lived in them woods, the man that lived in the shed, who wanted to build an underground tunnel to heaven, the one who told us about the black helicopters. That wasn't my daddy?"

"No, Odom."

"Who was he Momma?" My voice gets louder. I stand up.

"He was your step-daddy, Odom."

"Then what happened to *my* daddy, Momma? Where did he go?"

"Didn't go anywhere. Your real daddy died. See here," she hands two pieces of paper, official looking forms with notaries and signatures. It's a death certificate. I throw it to the ground and kick it out of my way. "I don't give a damn about any paperwork Momma. I want to know what happened."

"That's what I'm tryin' to show you. Thought maybe it'd be easier if you saw it for yerself. I can't think of any better way." Momma kneels to the floor and picks up the papers.

"How about you telling me, Momma."

"I just did."

"You didn't! You said he was dead."

"He did die, Odom. You were three years old. Birdshit was just about to be born. He worked for the Arkansas Western Railroad. He repaired broken trains. He was standing on top of a train he was fixing in one of the rail yards. There was an accident. Somehow the train he was standing on moved and he fell off the train. His head landed on the train tracks. He was in the hospital for three months. Then Birdshit was born. And it wasn't much longer after that when he died."

"I don't remember, Momma."

"I know you don't, Odom. You was too young. Can't you see what I'm tryin' to do here? This, these papers, these forms, the death certificate. This is very hard for me."

"I don't wanna see nothing Momma."

Momma lets go of the manila folder and 11x17 envelope and it falls to the floor. She doesn't bother looking to see where it fell. Or what spilled out. She crosses her arms, takes a deep breath and sits still.

"Then what Momma?"

"Then the Arkansas Western Railroad gave us a bunch of money. It was their fault. They gave us money and then Uncle Lou got a lawyer and sued the railroad and got us more money. That's why you never have to work if you don't want to. That's why when you bought your house Lou took care of it. That's why Lou takes care of everything. We've been living off the money from your daddy's death."

It doesn't even register fully. It sounds like she's talking about someone else.

I say, "Does Birdshit know this?"

"Yes."

"What?"

"I told her."

"When?"

"I don't know. Two years ago, three years ago. She was askin' questions. She knew something wasn't right. I told her and she promised not to say anything to you. I'm sorry. You seemed okay the way you saw things. The way it was in your mind. Your daddy was this mad genius who was too smart for his own good, too smart for the government, too smart for this world. You idolized him. I didn't want to take that away from you."

"I didn't idolize him, Momma."

I walk to the front door, pull back the curtain and find an empty spot in the front yard to focus on. "Then what happened to Daddy, the daddy I knew? Where is he?"

"Oh, Odom. Please don't tell me you don't remember."

"No, Momma, I don't."

"Oh, dear. Please don't make me bring this up." Her voice sounds like it's coming from the other end of a tunnel.

"Bring what up, Momma?"

"Please Odom. You remember. You have to remember."

"No, Momma. Tell me. What is it?"

"You remember, Odom. Don't make me tell it again."

"Where did Daddy go, Momma? What did he do? Tell me again."

"They took him away. They took him away."

I close my eyes. "Where, Momma? Where did they take him?" My voice is higher pitched than usual, softer, inquisitively childlike.

"To jail, then to the hospital in Little Rock, the mental hospital. That's where they took him."

"What did he do, Momma? Why'd they take him to jail? Why'd he go the hospital Momma? Was he crazy? Is that it?"

"Odom, he was crazy. They took him away." Her voice is wavering, the initial strength and confidence is gone. "I'm sorry, Odom. I didn't know."

"Didn't know what Momma? What didn't you know? Tell me again. I want to hear you tell me again."

I can no longer tell if my eyes are open or closed but I'm outside, standing in the front yard. I can see me through the curtains of the front door. I've pushed the curtains back to hide but I can still see me. "…didn't know what he was doing," Momma says in the background.

"What was he doing, Momma?" Even though I'm outside I can hear her voice, barely, but it's audible. I begin to walk towards the house. The curtains pull back and I see myself watching me walk closer and I can clearly see the look on my face. It's a look of disgust. I'm disgusted with myself.

"Out in them woods," her voice says. I step on the concrete front porch. I close the curtains. But I'm still there, hiding. I raise my right hand, make a fist and knock on the front door.

"What about them woods, Momma?"

"About him taking you and Birdshit back there."

"And what Momma?" I knock again, louder this time. The curtain draws back and I see myself watching me. I knock again and I step away from the curtain.

"His crazy stuff."

"Why did he take us back there, Momma?"

"Because, Odom."

"Because why, Momma? What did he do?"

"Goddamn Odom Shiloh! Goddamn it! Why do you want me to tell you this *again*?"

I raise both of my hands, ball them up into tight fists and punch the front door. Then I bring the underside of my fists hard onto the door, over and over again. I kick the door with my feet. "Momma!" I yell, kicking the door, "what did he do, Momma?"

"Odom, quit it! You're scaring me."

"Momma!" I punch, kick and pound my fists against the door in a loud, rhythmic pattern. Punch. Kick. Boom. Boom. Punch. Kick. Boom. Boom. "Momma. Can you hear me still?" Punch. Kick. Boom. Boom. "Tell me, Momma." Punch. Kick. Boom. Boom. The door rattles continuously, its hinges becoming more brittle with each assault. Punch. Kick. Boom. Boom. Momma's voice carries over the noise, "He took you and your sister out there in them woods."

"Yes, Momma?" Punch. Kick. Boom. Boom. "Then what?" With each kick, the door gives in more. "Then what, Momma?" Boom. Boom. Punch. Kick.

The door breaks open, dangling from the top hinge. There's no one behind the door. It's quiet. Quieter than it's ever been before. The door swings slightly, back and forth but I don't hear it. There is no sound, anywhere.

I walk into the house and still hear nothing. Momma is sitting in her chair, talking to me. Her mouth is moving, I can see the words created with her lips but no sound. She's talking to me like I'm understanding what she's saying. Momma. Momma. I can't hear my own voice. Momma. Momma. I feel my mouth moving but I can't make any sounds. No one can hear me. I can't hear anyone. The door continues to swing; I step out of the way and take slow steps, only moving one foot at a time, like I'm walking underwater. The closer I get to Momma, the more I see that she really thinks I can hear her. It's like she's telling me a story, a long story and I'm listening to her. The story is not a happy one, I can tell by the wrinkles under her eyes and the slope of her mouth when she pauses. Then she lets go of a file folder and envelope and it falls to the floor.

I see me.

I'm sitting on the couch, looking at Momma.

Then it becomes clear that she was not talking to me at all, she's talking to me on the couch. No one knows I'm here.

I don't exist.

I'm dead.

I'm sitting on the couch, my head cradled between my hands. I look exhausted. Momma continues to talk. Then I hear something. I lean in closer, only a few feet from Momma and I can barely hear her. It sounds like she's standing far away but I can hear her.

"Dr. Witten found out," she says. "He followed you all back there one day. He saw everything. He phoned Lou and Lou came down and the police showed up and then there was court and the hospital and I had to get a divorce. It was horrible. I had to drive to Little Rock and visit him in the hospital and pretend everything was okay for six months until his court date. That was the hardest six months of my life, Odom."

He saw everything.

What does that mean? I don't know. I try to talk. Momma. Momma. It doesn't work. No one knows I'm here. What does that mean? *He saw everything.*

I lean into Momma's ear and yell as loud as I can. What does that mean!

He saw everything.

There is no reaction.

She's no longer talking and I see that I continue to cradle my head in my hands, shaking it from side to side. I try again.

What does that mean? *He saw everything.*

She's looking off in the opposite direction, watching me on the couch.

Then she turns her head, slowly rotating it around and stops. She's looking straight ahead now.

He saw everything. What does that mean?

She turns her head even further until she's almost looking at me. I see her eyes move, up and down, scanning the room until they roam up towards my eyes and she's looking into my eyes. She's looking right at me, although there is no recognition in her gaze. She doesn't know I'm here. She has no idea I'm staring right back at her.

I think to myself—giving up on trying to use words—I think:

He saw everything. What does that mean?

She says, "It means he saw your daddy rape you, Odom."

Chapter Twenty Five

I OPEN MY EYES and I'm in the woods. It's dark and by the stiffness in my shoulders and knees, I've been out here awhile. I can see the night's sun in little rays through the trees. Before I have a chance to figure out what has happened I realize why I woke up. I hear voices. I hear someone calling my name. There are two people calling my name and then I see the beams from flashlights, crisscrossing the woods in front of me.

"Who is it?" I yell. The flashlights quit their jerky movements and stay still.

"Odom? Is that you?"

"Yeah." I brush the leaves off and stand up. "Over here," I yell again but not as loudly. My muscles feel like dried meat. Maybe I am getting older. I reach into my pocket and study the area around me as best I can but don't see my flashlight or shotgun. "Odom?" The voice says again. It's Blakey.

"I'm over here, Blakey." There's someone else behind him. Two flashlights pointed in my direction, their lights cutting, intersecting, getting momentarily lost in the chaos of the woods until they're both about twenty feet away and the lights, both of them land squarely on my face. I put my hands up, deflecting it.

"Sorry," Blakey says, dropping the yellow beam to the ground. "Let's get out of here Odom," he says, pointing with his other hand the direction to take.

I don't even ask what he's doing down here. Down in Arkansas. Down in Frothmouth. Down in the woods behind Momma's house. The other person has already turned around and begun the walk, taking the lead. Blakey asks if I'm okay and helps to brush me off. I ask what time it is and he says it's four in the morning. "Everybody's been worried," he says.

"Who is that?" I say, pointing.

"That's your sister. We drove down earlier today."

"What for?" I lose my step and fall to one knee. Blakey helps me up.

"Just because."

They walk me the rest of the way without asking any questions. We arrive at the house and Momma is standing by the front door in her robe under the porch light. She retells the events; how she told me everything and then I ran out of the house and then came back. And then ran off again for good. She called after me but I disappeared into the woods by myself with neither flashlight nor weapon. The more she called my name the faster I walked until I began to run. Turns out Birdshit and Blakey were at my house waiting for me and it wasn't until it got to be late that they began to worry and called Momma.

Momma didn't know they had driven down from Kansas City. So Blakey and my sister came over to Momma's and they went looking for me. Birdshit was confident they'd find me. She knows these woods like I do. She knows the path I would probably have taken without thinking and Birdshit was for the most part on the right path. They'd been looking for about an hour when they found me.

After the initial reunion conversation has subsided, Birdshit says, "We found him Momma, like always, sleeping out in them woods."

Blakey looks at her, pulls out his pack of Nuggets and slides out a lone cigarette. Momma asks if he'll go outside with that and Blakey says he planned on it but keeps his eye on Birdshit the whole time and says, "What you do mean always sleeping out there in them woods?"

"That's what Odom did all the time. He'd sleep out there."

"You mean even after everything that happened—" Blakey stops, but Birdshit finishes the thought with the answer. "Yep, even after everything. He could not not go out there. He was drawn to those woods. I don't know how to explain it. There's some kind of validation in re-creating, revisiting everything. Something happens to him out there."

I sit listening, not caring too much what their conversation is about, although I know it's about me. And finally after fifteen more minutes of this, I get a little fed up and ask them what in the hell they're doing down here. Birdshit spouts off about needing some of her things. She and Michael are getting a place together in

Kansas City. They've even been talking about marriage. She had to leave Michael behind, obviously; he's still wanted. I nod my head without much reaction.

"Lou's on his way down," Blakey says, "he'll be here later."

"What for?"

"He's taking you to Memphis."

"Oh, shit." I remember everything all at once.

Everyone around me tries to act normal. They make breakfast and comment on the morning news. They watch game shows and guess at the puzzles. Birdshit works on a poem and Blakey dodges outside every ten minutes to smoke a cigarette and make a phone call. Everyone knows about Memphis. Everyone knows that the guy who collided with me or I ran over or however it happened died and everyone knows that I have to go to Memphis and turn myself in. They've been looking for me. I've been very lucky the past few days; they haven't been back to Frothmouth. But it would be no time before someone in Frothmouth tells the wrong person that I'm back and they come pick me up in a dark blue four door sedan with U.S. Government plates and black helicopters hovering overhead to take me where no one would ever see me again—just the way I thought they took Daddy away.

I don't think I really understood it yet. But the more I think back, I think that what happened in them woods occurred in a place that only Daddy, me and Birdshit resided in and we were the only three who were to know that we existed there. I'll tell you something else; it's not like in the movies or on the television what he did to us. I really can't tell you what it is. There's no word for it. Even if there was, I don't think I could say it. But I suppose the easiest way to think of it is to imagine the stillest quiet in the world, maybe a graveyard at night. And then think of the greatest distance you can conjure up in your mind and combine the two. It's like opening a secret door to the end of the universe and following it further and further away until you can stop and watch yourself from behind. And there isn't another soul alive at that very moment, there's not a loneliness on this earth that can match it. Even god looks the other way.

I can't help but think about how conventional wisdom might lead one to suspect we're closer because of our experience. Truth is, we don't want to be close to anyone. Birdshit and I will live and die brother and sister but we'll never be able to heal and mend the little gaps, the tiny worlds we have to live in by ourselves. The silence of the other while the one was claimed.

Blakey pokes his face inside, an arch of smoke climbs over his head and drifts into the living room. "Lou's here!" I can't help but smile. Lou does that to people. When he walks in the front door, I get up and give him a big handshake and he wraps his arms around me. My Uncle Lou. My read Daddy's brother. This is the closet I'll ever be to my father.

Momma brings coffee and warmed sweet rolls and slabs of butter into the living room. Lou indulges, lathering the rolls in a luxuriant golden glow of melted butter. It looks marvelous, like something the ancients worshipped. Lou eats them methodically, one roll at a time, three bites to each roll. I sip my coffee and listen.

Lou sits down in the guest chair. He carefully explains that there are several different scenarios that may take place. "First of all, they will place you under arrest. Be ready for that. However, I may be able to immediately bail you out or it may take a few hours. Worst case scenario, you have to spend the night in jail and I'll get you out first thing the next morning. That's doubtful but possible."

"Okay," I say, realizing I have no control in this matter.

"It ain't that bad," Blakey says.

"Right," Lou says, turning around. "Blakey here can tell you all about jail. Not a big deal at all is it, Blakey?"

"No, sir."

"Anyhow, like I was saying, whatever they throw our way we can handle."

"Then what?"

"Well, it depends what they charge you with for starters. It depends on a lot of things. Depends on who I can call, who I can get in touch with. Let me worry about those things. You just be polite, yes sir, no sir."

"When do we leave?"

"Whenever you're ready."

Chapter Twenty Six

I CLOSED MY EYES when we left Momma's house. Blakey rode up front in the passenger seat while Lou drove. The last thing I remembered was Lou talking on his cell phone.

And when I open my eyes I can see downtown Memphis just coming into view and the bridge we'll have to cross. The other side of the great river. I thought I would never be back. I had vowed to never set foot in Tennessee again. But I know Lou is right. I have to turn myself in. I have to face up to it or else I'll never rid myself of it. They'd find me, eventually they would. I don't know what Lou has up his sleeves but I'm hoping the best damn lawyer in Memphis and a plea deal I can't refuse await me on the other side of that bridge.

We're downtown on Front Street and Lou navigates like a pro. Before I know it he's stopped, gotten out of the car, told Blakey to go park and is walking me inside the police station. I don't even have time to look up and read the letters on the outside of the building. Lou walks up to a window where a police officer is sitting on the other side.

"I called earlier and spoke with Detective Achmed. My name's Lou Shiloh."

The police officer dials an extension and informs the detective that Lou is here. A minute later a door opens and the detective and a uniformed officer holding a pair of cuffs approach. Lou extends his hand to shake and Achmed points to me and says, "This is him?" Lou nods his head. Detective Achmed gives the uniformed officer a look and he tells me to turn around with my hands behind my back.

I'm cuffed, escorted away, fingerprinted, photographed and handcuffed to a bench in the hallway. Down to my left is where the jail is. Orange-suited inmates are led in and out of this metal door down that way. To my right is where I came from, the front door, the offices. I sit for thirty minutes, maybe more. I can't tell. An hour could've passed and I wouldn't know it. Then the reality of prison settles on me like fresh sawdust that's been floating through the air. I think about all those things you hear about prison life, the rapes, the assaults, the violence. The damage you confront daily. I'm sure prison is full of victims. One way or another we all end up in the same place. It comes full circle.

Detective Achmed comes over and unhooks me from the bench.

"My friend, come." I begin to walk to my left.

"This way," he says. I follow him back the way I came in. We pass through the same door. Lou and Blakey are standing there. Behind me Detective Achmed is jingling some keys and then I feel him pull off the handcuffs.

"Ready?" Lou says.

"For what?"

"Head on back."

"I'm done?"

"Yes."

"That's it?"

"That's it," Lou says, opening the door for me. We walk outside, a gust of wind blows Lou's hair over to the wrong side. He pushes it back down where it belongs.

Blakey is standing outside like a sentry, working on a Nugget. Blakey jogs down the street and disappears. Lou rubs his belly, says something about more sweet rolls and coffee. We wait for Blakey.

"When do I come back?" I say.

"You don't."

"But when's my court date?"

"You don't have one."

Blakey pulls up, puts the SUV in park and Lou walks over to the driver's side.

"What do I do now?" I say, getting in the back seat.

"You're a free man," Blakey says, lighting a Nugget, rolling down the window.

"The hell you talking about?"

"It's over."

"What's over?"

Lou clears his throat. We both go quiet. Lou drives us out of downtown Memphis, gets us over the bridge and back into Arkansas. Once we pass the Southland Greyhound Track and settle into a cruise control speed Lou speaks up again.

"Odom. Everything is taken care of. You were placed under arrest back there for a misdemeanor charge, a fine was issued. It was paid and now it's over."

"But the guy died, Lou."

"It wasn't your fault, Odom."

"I know it wasn't."

"Well, then why should you have to face exaggerated charges?"

"How did you do this?"

"The coroner could not positively determine what caused Pierre's death. Could have been an accident. A faulty safety helmet. A pre-existing condition."

"What kind of pre-existing condition?"

"I don't know if there was one. I'm just saying there could've been one. Anyhow, I made a few phone calls; I've been working on this. I didn't know what agreement would be accepted or what would happen when we got to Memphis but I had a pretty good feeling things would work out the way they should. They did want to know what you were doing in Memphis in the first place. They keep you in suspense like this. Best thing to do is say nothing. Give them a carrot and do what they tell you afterwards."

"I don't even remember," I say.

"I know you don't. I told them things haven't been going well for you lately. That you've sorta lapsed back into this fit you get into sometimes. When you disengage and stay away from people and stare off, wander around, sleep outside."

"I don't sleep."

Lou steers with one hand and Blakey stares straight ahead as we roll onward. Several minutes pass, maybe ten or so when Lou looks at Blakey and nods his head. Blakey turns around in his seat to face me.

"Odom. I don't know how to tell you this but we think it'd be best if you moved back in with your Momma. Maybe you should sell your house. We think," he looks at Lou, then back at me, "that it's becoming too much for you."

"What do you mean?"

"Well, this condition of yours, for starters. Bree has talked to us a few times about you, how things have kind of spiraled downward for you."

"What the hell did she say?"

"No, no. It's not like that. Just think about it, that's all we're saying. Might be good for you to move in with your Momma again. You probably belong there."

"Where's my sister gonna live?"

Lou adjusts his rearview so that I can see his eyes in it. He says, "She'll stay in Kansas City. I'll help her out up there. She'll be fine."

For a flashing moment anger burns through me and then it's gone and I smile and laugh out loud. Loud enough for Blakey to turn around and Lou to watch me through the rearview.

I say, "Is this how it's supposed to work out?"

"I think so," Blakey says.

"That's crazy."

Blakey says, "No, it's the Shiloh way, Odom."

"Momma said all those things about the Shilohs was delusional nonsense that Daddy imagined."

"No, not exactly. Some of it is true," Blakey says, lighting a fresh cigarette.

"Which parts?"

"The Shiloh part."

"What about the Shiloh's? You mean like what Lou just did for me?"

"Maybe."

"Maybe what?"

"You tell me."

"What do you really do, Blakey, huh?"

Lou says, "I'll tell you what he does."

"What's that?" I say.

"He does good work. That's why he's always been around. Why he'll always be around, Odom. Blakey's never going away."

"What do you mean why he's always been around. I hadn't seen Blakey in years."

"It hasn't been that long, Odom. You see him more than you think."

"Okay," I say. "Whatever you say." There's nothing else I can think of to ask them.

I shake my head after a minute of deliberate silence. Lou is watching me in the rearview. Blakey peers back at me in between drags on his cigarette and flicks the ash out the window. I give up. "I'm not going to get anything out of y'all, am I?"

"Not much."

"Blakey. Please at least tell me that you were never a hitman."

"If that were true I can say that I've done worse things in my life than that."

"Is it true?"

No answer. More glances through the rearview, more cigarettes, more smoke in my eyes, more miles on the odometer.

After awhile I say, "So what's next for you, Blakey?"

"Going back up to KC. Settle down with Trisha. Become a stand-up comedian."

"A what…" I drop it. "And you, Lou?"

"Open up my new restaurant in Overland Park. Get your sister and Michael working there and maybe some day get you and your Momma to leave Frothmouth behind and come up to Kansas City with everybody. One big happy family. You could help run one of the restaurants."

"You lost me on the one big happy family part, Lou."

He doesn't hear me and neither does Blakey. They're hypnotized by the hum of the wheels on the road. I close my eyes and imagine Blakey on a municipal stage somewhere in Minnesota yapping about being a good ol' boy from the south and how life is so funny up north.

I imagine Lou's BBQ opening to rave reviews. I can see him in a different booth, still reading his *Star*, watching over the place and still wondering if there is or isn't a secret basement at the original Lou's BBQ.

I guess at how long it will be before Birdshit wants nothing more to do with Michael and comes back down to Arkansas. I give it three months. Hell, if she makes it three months, that'd be good for her. Eventually Michael will have to come back and face his charges too. But I'm sure Lou will work something out, in the way Lou always does.

As for Bree, the divorce is what it is. But I love her, I can't help it. She's one of us. I have to protect her—at least, I feel like I have to. I got wind of what that good-for-nothing David Garner did to her the other night. Momma told me in the living room when we were talking yesterday. Said David broke her arm, bruised her up and assaulted her. She wouldn't tell me what she meant by assaulting.

I have one more thing left to do.

I read the sign that welcomes us to Franks County and I know we'll be home real soon. I let my eyelids drop, feeling the wind from Blakey's window brush up against my face, smiling to myself as I return beyond sleep, beyond reach. I know exactly where that shotgun is and I know exactly where I can find that David Garner and I know exactly what spot in them woods where he's going to live out the rest of his life. Once, the Shiloh Foundation took him on as a contract employee. He did a high-order job for the Shilohs, burning down that shed, filling in that hole. Such a good job, in fact, that I think the time's ripe for permanent employment. And I can feel the thumping in my chest, the faint sound of the helicopters approaching. Soon they'll be overhead, circling and waiting for me.

39427420R00129

Made in the USA
Lexington, KY
22 February 2015